MASHA'ALLAH AND OTHER STORIES

ABOUT THE JAMES D. HOUSTON AWARD

Known as a masterful writer in both fiction and nonfiction genres, James D. Houston was also a dedicated teacher and passionate promoter of emerging authors. Friends and family have established a fund to honor his memory and further his legacy. The James D. Houston Award will support publication of books by writers who reflect Jim's humane values, his thoughtful engagement with life, and his literary exploration of California, Hawai'i, and the West. For more information about the award and how to donate to it and submit a manuscript for consideration, please visit www.heydaybooks.com/houstonaward/.

MASHA'ALLAH

and Other Stories

MARIAH K. YOUNG

HEYDAY, BERKELEY, CALIFORNIA

LIBRARY OF CONGRESS
CATALOGING-IN-PUBLICATION DATA

Young, Mariah K.

Masha'allah and other stories / Mariah K. Young.

p. cm.

ISBN 978-1-59714-203-8 (pbk. : alk. paper) —

ISBN 978-1-59714-213-7 (apple e-book) —

ISBN 978-1-59714-207-6 (amazon kindle e-book) —

ISBN 978-1-59714-212-0 (hardcover : alk. paper)

1. Oakland (Calif.)—Fiction. I. Title.

PS3625.O96726M37 2012

813'.6—dc23

2012008018

Cover Design: Lorraine Rath
Interior Design/Typesetting: Joe Lops
Printing and Binding: Thomson-Shore, Dexter, MI

Orders, inquiries, and correspondence should be addressed to:

Heyday

P.O. Box 9145, Berkeley, CA 94709

(510) 549-3564, Fax (510) 549-1889

www.heydaybooks.com

10 9 8 7 6 5 4 3 2 1

CONTENTS

"Work is love made visible."

—KHALIL GIBRAN

MR. FELIX

THICK FEBRUARY FOG the day they put Mr. Felix to rest, but not so thick we couldn't feel the sun through the haze. It was late on Saturday morning, and there were lots of folks out. No cars on the street. We never saw the street cleared out, and we didn't know better, so we got a game of football going. I had a bright green NERF ball, brand new, no scuffs or foam chunks missing yet. My cousins and I and a few kids from the block split into teams, and we ran passes up and down the street, scoring touchdowns once you passed the broken fire hydrant at the corner. I was about to throw a spiral down the block when they shouted at us. They never talked to us kids unless they had to. But that day Enzo called my name. "Dylan, get your ass out the street!"

We ran to the curb. They lined us up against the bumper of Londell's dark blue Monte Carlo. I dropped the ball and slid on top of the hood, just like all the block boys do when they're posted. Enzo pointed his Fritos bag down toward our hands. Londell didn't pay us mind except to say, "Don't go jumping on the hood." Marcus took my little cousin Edina and put her on his shoulders. She pulled at his dreads, but Marcus just bounced a little on the heels of his Chucks until she laughed, let go, and rested her hands on top of his head.

Funerals are ordinary. Processions happen all the time. But I'd never seen one where our street, which was always buzzing, was completely still. Up and down the block, people came out of front doors and off porches to stand at the curb. Even the old folks who never came out and the crackheads who could barely stand up were there. A horse-drawn carriage appeared at the mouth of East Fourteenth and turned. Two horses, both white with gray manes, clip-clopped down the concrete, pulling a box piled high with red and white roses. The casket was there for everyone to see, light brown with golden rails, like my ma's hair, almost like mine.

Londell said, "There he goes. Mr. Felix."

The carriage wheels turned, making this creaky little noise as the casket went by. The flowers shook when the casket crossed a crack or a pothole.

The hustlers bowed their heads. "Waste of talent," Enzo said, cracking his knuckles. Marcus said the casket was lined with Italian silk and thousand-dollar bills. They stopped talking. Everyone did.

Behind the carriage came a stream of Rolls-Royces and Bentleys, all gold and creamy, shining like they just came off the lot. I stopped counting after twenty. Each car had bundles of red roses arranged along the front and back bumpers. In the cabs, women were in fur coats with little boys and girls on their laps, and men were in black suits. They stared at us behind dark sunglasses.

No more Mr. Felix. I was a small fry, and even I knew his name. It was the kind of thing you know without really knowing, how everyone got made or got paid through him. I'd seen him. He always wore clean suits with iron lines down the legs. The only Mister I knew about. Ma told me never to run around with anyone who talked about him too much, said there were other ways to live. Then she'd go to work. I kept the TV on all night. If it was off when I woke up in the morning, she was home.

Mr. Felix got caught up, sent to Leavenworth, and stabbed in his cell. The newspapers said he died over a five-dollar debt. Ma said good riddance when she heard the news, but she came out like everybody else and stood in front of our place. She'd wrapped up her hair in red, and her face was like the statue of the Mexican Virgin by our school, smooth and calm, her mouth hard.

For once there were no voices on a block that could never shut up. Some women were crying a little, but most people just watched. Some folks nodded, raised their arms, or flashed their signs. A woman yelled out, "The sword of Jesus is long and broad!" She was an old lady who had been on this block for always, since my ma was a kid. Mrs. Patterson. A group of people tried to send her into her house, and first she pushed one of them away, but soon she let them walk her to her porch. She appeared in her window. She watched the procession and held her hands tight.

The block was always loud with beat boxes and car engines and people jocking. But when Mr. Felix rolled through, even as a dead man, it was quiet. I could hear birds and traffic from far away. The wind even had a sound, a low whistle that hooked on the horse's hair, picked the petals off the bouquets and sent them on their way to the ground. I watched Marcus and Londell and Enzo follow that procession with their eyes, and I slid off the car hood. I looked at the neighborhood, everyone out, and my ma saw me standing with them. She reached out her hand for me to come to her, but she didn't call out. Her arm stayed there.

I would have gone over, stood beside her, but Enzo rubbed the top of my head and told me to straighten up. I could smell his leather jacket. I hooked my thumb into the belt loop of my jeans. The Rolls kept rolling by, and I caught our reflection in a passing window.

ONE SPACE

N ORMALLY, THE ALARM wakes you, rouses you out of dream darkness. But this morning it is the ache that cracks the black of sleep, a gash on your left hip, just above your belt line, still fresh from yesterday. You keep your eyes closed. Focus on the dark, ignore the slight burn and linger in that haze, those last few moments of quiet. The dark folds and collapses, and you almost feel yourself fall back until Felipe twitches next to you. Your eyelids tighten, then flap open. Whether you like it or not, you're awake. Felipe keeps shifting, shakes the whole bed. Once you were the restless one, always moving in the throes of sleep. Eldie, your wife, always complained about it, but in the mornings, early like now, she would find your body in the dark, fit her arm under yours and her knees into yours, her forehead pressed to your shoulder. Only then would you stay put. Now, every morning you wake up in the same position you fell asleep in.

The clock says 4:47 in red digital letters. Felipe is still asleep beside you, sprawled on his back and his head half hanging off the bed. His boots are still on, untied but still tightly laced. Filthy Felipe, your bedmate for the last two months. When you two first arrived, you joked about how the two of you were packed onto this twin bed like sardines, that the only way you'd fit is if you both made like fishes, one man's feet beside the other's head at night. The joke has lost most of its steam, but it manages a smile out of you both at night, your feet by his ears and his by yours, too tired to complain about the smell or the narrow space between.

Morning is just behind the hills. The others are stirring awake, anticipating the bleating alarm. Luis and Leo share a bed on the other side of the garage, and Nestor sleeps on the couch along the wall. Nestor is Felipe's second cousin from somewhere back in Sinaloa. That's how you ended up here, because you knew Felipe in Los Angeles, and he told you about the construction in the bay. Word of mouth and people back home, phone calls and favors—a haphazard but more or less reliable mode of finding work and shelter.

You pay one hundred dollars to share this mattress with Felipe and chip in twenty a week for food: rice, pintos, coffee, eggs and flank steak and onions, mangoes and oranges when the price is right. Everything else goes into a money order bound for a market in Poza Rica. The money is for a new room on your father's house and for your sister Marielena's tuition to a Catholic high school in Mexico City. And your wife Edelmira, Eldie. You rub your face and roll off the bed. In the bathroom, you wash up and grab your work clothes from a nail on the wall.

Under the white bulb, you examine the electrical tape covering the cut. Inspecting the cut will tear the scab, so you leave the tape be. Yesterday, you hauled new toilets up five flights of stairs to be installed in renovated lofts. On one of your trips, your hip snagged on a nail jutting from an exposed beam, and you almost dropped the toilet you carried. The wound yawns an inch across, jagged like a crooked smile, but not deep enough to need stitches. After work, Nestor helped you salve the wound with Vaseline and seal the flaps of skin shut with gauze and tape. Looking makes it itch, and you hope it's the itch that comes with scabbing and healing.

Nestor is making breakfast on the single gas burner set on a crate beside a small brown refrigerator. Water boils for coffee. Tortillas warm over a blue flame. Nestor scoops scrambled eggs into tortillas, wraps them and stacks them on a plate, grabs one and sits on his couch to eat. The smells coax everyone up, and each man takes a turn stammering in and out of the bathroom, rubbing sore legs and stiff backs in the low morning light. It is far too early for words, only nods and groans, the language of the waking.

Everyone pulls sweatshirt hoods over their heads, tightens their bootlaces. You finish the last grainy bit of coffee in your cup and follow the others out the back door and through the neighborhood, still sleeping. It is vaguely dark when you all leave the house at 5:15. Up to East Twelfth three blocks over, then up another two to the Jornalero Zone adjacent to High Street. The dark blue of night is bleeding into purple and faint yellow at the hills.

Felipe trots next to you, rubbing his eyes. "Nes, when you gonna stop brewing battery acid and calling it coffee?" He's the first to talk in just about any situation, and usually for better rather than worse.

"When you get up and make breakfast, you make the coffee however you please," Nestor says over his shoulder.

"And rob the boys of your eggs? How could I?" Felipe picks up his speed, nudges Nestor's back with his elbow. "Your cooking redeems you."

Nestor breaks away from the group at International Boulevard;

he made friends with a contractor from Piedmont, who comes to pick up Nestor at 5:30 sharp. They work landscaping in the hills and sometimes in Marin. Nestor makes eighty dollars straightaway, ten dollars an hour and full days most of the time. Landscaping doesn't sound so bad. Running a dust blower and trimming bushes seem fine compared to pounding nails and tarring roofs. But you could make twice what Nestor makes in a day if you can get on the right crew and head to the right site. Or you could make nothing at all if the trucks are slow that day, or if it rains, or if the contractor doing the picking doesn't like your face.

Dawn at East Twelfth and High. A long row of pier storage warehouses, dusty pink on their way to white gray. A city sign on the corner spells it out: DAY LABOR HIRING ZONE, ZONA DE TRABAJAR. Cars are few and far between, their headlamps muted in the morning fog. The only lights are from these cars and the streetlamps and the sky in that uneasy time between night and day.

Dotting street corners and cement slabs and retaining walls and concrete truck ports, men wait in clusters and alone, eyes on the street and hands rubbing fast against the morning cold. Baseball hats and flannel sweaters, boots and pant legs splattered with paint. Some wear backpacks and tool belts; a few have muscle belts for lifting. They wait for a pickup or a van to slow along the curb, for the contractors to pull up alongside a crew and shout out how many they need this morning: ten men, three men, twenty men, one.

In your left pocket, six dollars for lunch. In your right, a plastic phone card good for forty-three minutes and a phone number for the market on a side street in Poza Rica, the closest market with a pay phone. Later tonight at six o'clock in Oakland and eight o'clock in Poza Rica, Eldie will be there waiting for your call. And you can't wait to make the call. More than anything, you want to hear her voice, catch the sound of her breath hitting the receiver, and pretend it is hitting your neck. The closest thing is her voice through wire, stretched over a thousand miles of distance. It's as close as you get in the fifteen months since you left with three other men from Poza Rica.

In your breast pocket is your newest ID. You've accumulated several in your travels: social security and identity cards, two for California. Each has a different city of residence, a different age, a different name. Jose Tercera in Phoenix, where you mopped hotel floors during the night shift. Ezekiel Orozco in Los Angeles, where you cut up chunks of fresh fish at a Japanese restaurant. Now, you are Raymond Ortega, but you haven't needed to show your newest card to any of the men who hire you to build houses or tear them down. The picture is the same for all of them, you looking sheepishly at the camera lens in the pharmacy photo booth, black hair slicked back, and your skin sallow against the blue background curtain.

You stand against a concrete building, close enough to the corner that should a work truck come along, you won't have to sprint to wave the driver down, only jog. You nod to some of the men you see every morning. Luis and Leo and you lean against the wall, while Felipe walks back and forth on the edge of the curb.

"We should try for San Jose," Felipe says after a while. "Tommy said there's some good money down there. High-rises going up."

"Tommy who?" Luis pipes up.

"Tommy at the Gato Negro. The bartender. He told me there

are crews down in San Jose getting four hundred for two days' work. We could get in on that."

Luis spat. "I was down there for a while, couldn't get anything regular. All them big contractors got their own people. They only want us for the small shit. Ain't worth it."

You shift from one foot to the other. "What does Tommy know? He back behind the bar pouring drafts all day." You've heard Tommy talk. Tommy will tell you whatever will get him a tip.

"He listens, dumb ass," Felipe says and pulls at the string of his hoodie. "That's his job, to overhear shit. He hears things, and he tells me."

"He tells you about jobs somewhere else to get you out of his bar," Luis chuckles. Leo chuckles too. Felipe flips them off, and they return matching birds. Felipe looks out at the street, watches cars pass by on the thoroughfare toward the highway on-ramp. He's getting the itch for new scenery, you can tell, and he's getting tired of Luis telling him to be patient. He has been talking about news of a resort development in the Sierras. You like the idea. You told Eldie about the resort the last time you talked to her two weeks ago, how you were excited to see the mountains and the snow. You have never seen snow. "But you hate the cold," she had said, her voice wavering just enough for you to notice.

A white flatbed truck pulls up to the curb. The driver holds up his hand, all fingers spread. Five men. He points haphazardly into the throng, who hustle from down the block. The man's extended finger passes over you. Felipe hops into the back of the truck with the others, some faces you recognize and others you don't. That's how it goes, some old faces, and every day some new ones.

You were new to this block not long ago, but this block isn't very different from Dupont Street in Phoenix where you were last spring, or Vermont Avenue in Los Angeles during the summer. You found a space to stand and a few men you could call friends. You only came to Oakland because Felipe told you about the new complexes going up, how his cousins were making one hundred and fifty bucks a day, cash. There was even an extra space in the truck that Felipe was riding in to the Bay Area. It almost makes you smile, how more and more that's all you need in this life—one space in the truck.

This time a van pulls up, and the others jog to the curb with arms raised. "Movers! Movers! Dos hombres!" the man shouts from the driver's seat, holding up two fingers for all to see.

You rush to the van doors and jump in when they unlock; you know the other man who makes it into the van, Chavez, from a construction job when you first came to Oakland. You nod at each other, waiting for the van to pull away. Right place at the right time. That's how it goes, whether you work or not. If you're at the right corner, you work. The man turns to the two of you and says in halted Spanish that you'll move furniture in Alameda, two hours, fifty dollars. You both nod, and the van pulls away. It is 7:20.

YOU LOOK AT the box spring and then the stairwell and then back at the box spring, considering its height and the narrowness of the hallway. The bed is the last thing to go up. The boxes and chairs were carried up to the third-floor apartment with relative ease. The stairwell and the wooden box spring, however, have presented a challenge. The young man who picked you up is looking at his watch and then at you. He has only so much cash, you can tell, and you want to get the bed upstairs before the whole morning is gone and you won't be able to find another crew for the day. You look to Chavez, who rubs his chin thoughtfully.

"Chingado, let's force it," he says, and you agree. Grabbing the front corner, you pull the plastic wrapped mattress off the pavement and wait for Chavez to pick up the rear. By the second landing, your grip is starting to give, and your lower back flares. A mattress corner knocks the ceiling, takes bits of white plaster off as it rounds the corner, but the landing is in sight. You pull the box spring up in a final grunt, your fingers about to buckle in the heat and pull of heavy plastic. It's easier now to push it down the hallway through the apartment door and into the bedroom. The man, who hovered behind as you and Chavez lumbered the boxes and furniture up those flights of stairs, says thank you several times and hands each of you two twenties and a ten, and then opens the door, as if you are a guest being shown out. It's then that you realize he isn't giving you a ride back. You stuff the money in your pocket and leave silently; in the hallway, you kick the chipped wall where the box spring created a crack. A little chunk falls down the stairs as you exit the building.

The two of you catch the bus back. The clock on the bus says 8:54, and you are hopeful there will still be trucks circling. You rub the ache out of your hands and discreetly check the gash on your hip. The wound is slightly swollen and pink around the border of tape, but you decide it's not infected. It's already starting to heal, you decide, but as soon as you pull the waistband of your sweatshirt over it, the pain flickers and radiates through your hip and down your leg. Chavez sees you tense with the pain and then relax, but he says nothing about it. "What a jack-off job that was," he offers.

You agree—you want to make more than fifty dollars today ($48.25 after the bus ride). After getting off the bus, you and Chavez find a good spot to wait in a muffler shop parking lot a block away from the intersection of the Zone. Other men are still out; you all trade looks and nods, then all eyes turn back to the street.

After maybe an hour, a red truck pulls along the curb. You and Chavez and a few others rush toward the van. The driver peers out at you from the truck cab; he wears sunglasses that reflect in rainbows, and he never takes his hand off the steering wheel. "Cuatro para construcción!" he says, and waits for the first four to jump in the truck bed. You hunker down on a wheel well and pull your sweatshirt hood tight around your neck. It's almost ten o'clock, and the morning cold wears on you, breathing down on you hard as the truck picks up speed. High Street flows by you, now filled with people and cars and the sounds of the waking world.

You arrive at a construction site in the Oakland hills, where new sets of condominiums are going up beside the freeway. The first set of buildings is already complete, all in alternating shades of beige and cinnamon and tan. The truck bounces past the sapling-lined streets dotted with minivans to an unpaved road, where the condos rise out of fresh concrete foundations.

Today, your job is to fill in the skeletal wood beams with insulation and plaster, to make this house frame into a home for a family to live in. Beyond the open square of the kitchen, there are intermittent sounds of hammering and the occasional shout for the foreman. The boom box on the ledge sputters hip-hop.

A buzz saw screams somewhere on the ground floor, its high-pitched whine cutting your eardrum. Packing insulation into what will soon be a kitchen wall, you look at the holes and pencil marks for the dishwasher and the kitchen island and imagine Eldie spinning across the finished room, high heels click-clacking across the hardwood floor. On top of every burner would be a pot simmering with something delicious. She would love this window, the bright blue sky cutting into the hills. You can almost hear her voice crack into a squeak when she says, "This is the perfect place for a table, right here where we can see the view." She would smile and run her hand along the ridge of your shoulders, and a rise of gooseflesh scampers over you for a second as you turn to grab another handful of insulation.

You look around this half-ready house and remind yourself of the new room in your father's house being built, how it will be your parents' bedroom apart from your brother and his wife and their children. It seems there is always a new baby born or another on the way every time you call home. Whenever you speak with your brothers, they have news of some cousin or neighbor or friend with a new baby.

The foam thread clings to your hands like spiderwebs, thin and elusive as that thought in the dark or in those long stretched-out moments of waiting: You already know you are more valuable away from home than in it, but do they rely on it? No, they do not dread your return. But to come home without something to offer—best not to come home at all. The score is clear: back in Poza Rica, you wouldn't be working at all. You would never be able to have a home for you and Eldie. You would be in the living room of your father's house still, your part cordoned off by a sheet hung over a rope, just enough room for you and Eldie to sleep. Here, in the United States, in this half-built home with insulation packing in your hands, you are useful. The money you send puts food in mouths, puts money in Eldie's pocket, and sends Marielena to school. It builds a new room for your parents. The cut sears when you bend to grab another section of padding. You hold your breath when you twist to grab more.

By one o'clock the fog has long since burned away and the sun has come out, bright as ever. The contractor signals all the men to break for lunch. On the open gate of the contractor's truck bed, you sit and survey the houses pushing up from the hills. The contractor has brought sandwiches wrapped in cellophane in a bright red ice chest. He tosses a bologna sandwich and a store-brand cola to each of the men. He points to his watch. "Una hora, hombres."

You eat and watch the cars along the highway inch farther and farther toward the bridge. Today the water is calm and blue, darkest at the deepest parts. Your father had a small boat that he took out in the bay to catch white fish, fat tilapia with gaping mouths. He had traps for mussels and blue-bellied crabs. Your father should have been a tour guide for the tourists in Vera-cruz. You used to tell him to take them on fishing tours, take them clamming along the beaches. But he had no heart for it. He didn't like people enough for that kind of thing. It was more that he didn't have the money to bribe the men who give out permits and licenses for such ventures. Your father took his fish to market and lived modestly. A skill is a gold piece that will never fall out of your pocket, he used to say.

In fifteen months, you've picked up many skills. You know how to tear out old carpet. You know how to reinforce a weight-bearing wall, and you know the weak points to aim for when breaking one down. You know how to scale a whole yellowfin without breaking the delicate flesh along its belly. You know how to lay tile and clean away leftover scraps of grout. You know how to tell time through the body—two hours have passed when the ache in your right shoulder blade returns, another hour when that pain begins to work its way up to your neck.

The first thing you ever built was a door frame when you were eight. Your father had finished the new back door of your house, and he called you over, showed you how you measure wood planks with a string, a pencil, and a careful finger. You think of patching drywall and nail-gunning wood beams together. You think about pouring concrete. You think about shiny bathroom fixtures, brass pipes, curtain rods. Your father built his home himself, constructed it from floor to roof, put in every new room and fixture. You have only built walls, front steps, doorways, hallways, stairs, and closets, rooms for others to fill.

IT IS ALMOST five when the contractor tells you to wrap it up, that you all did good work today. You push the last bit of foam into the wall and dust yourself off. You're covered in the thin threads of insulation packing, and you roll your hands across the thighs of your jeans. The threads spin into twisted strands, sprigs of pale yellow strings. The contractor sits in the truck cab and peels twenties off a roll; he comes over with the bills sectioned off for each of you. He hands you three twenties, ten dollars for each hour worked. The bills are soft and crumpled, worn from passing between so many hands before arriving in yours. You tuck them in your back pocket and climb into the back of the truck.

The ride back to the Zone takes a while. The cut on your hip keeps rubbing against the waistband of your jeans; the tape and gauze patch will need to be replaced when you get back to the garage. The man drops you at the same corner where he picked you up, waves good-bye as he pulls away. He was a good boss. He paid you what you earned, gave you lunch and time to eat it. He put on the banda station while you all ate together. You prefer merengue, but you appreciated the gesture.

You walk to the market on Thirty-fifth Avenue because it has pay phones in the back lot, away from the sounds of traffic and people moving about the city. The last clock you saw said it was 5:52, and long enough has passed so that time must be crowding into six, if not already there. You imagine Eldie sitting in one of the plastic chairs outside the shop. You see her in jeans and a red shirt, her black hair down—this is always how you imagine her, out in the world anyway. That's what she wore when you first took her out; you watched an American movie about aliens with no subtitles, and the two of you made up the dialogue at the more exciting parts and spent the slower screen time kissing.

You fish out your phone card and dial the numbers, key in your pin, and enter the market number. It rings and rings and rings.

"Hello?" The voice is coarse, low. "Speak!"

"Eldie?" You hesitate. The phone clicks dead. You hang up and try again. The same voice sounds through the receiver.

"Who is this?"

"Who is *this?* I'm calling for Edelmira Sena." Your voice gets loud.

"Clear the line." The voice on the other end is gravelly, grumbling. "I'm waiting for a call."

"No, I'm on now. My wife—" This should be much simpler.

"Get off the line. My sister is about to call." She hangs up on you again. You imagine a fat woman, old and sour. Moles on her chin with hairs springing out of them. An old bag with a mean cane. Probably likes to hit children with it.

You redial. This time, no one answers. You try again and again until you practically memorize the pattern of numbers across the grid of one to zero, your fingers crossing each followed by a jab on the pound sign. You try different strategies. At first you wait a few minutes and call back. Then you double-check the number and dial it successively. Each time, the hollow sound of the ringing tone buzzes in the phone. Finally, the phone clicks back to life. Another voice comes on. It's a man's voice, and you don't recognize his dialect—something Indian. "Get off the line!" you shout, but the voice keeps jabbering, and you finally slam the phone back in its cradle.

At first, you try not to be angry. This is the number a lot of jornaleros use to call home. Sometimes a row of people waits to use the phone, waiting for their husband or brother or sister or son or daughter to call. Scenarios, explanations arrange themselves in your mind. Eldie stuck in the middle of the phone line, deciding whether to be polite and wait, or tell the old wench hogging the phone to get off the line, her husband is about to call. You think of the stretch from your house to the market, a half hour's walk through the valley to the paved roads of the square. The winter rains could be falling, and maybe the road is blocked or too deep with mud to pass. There, in her red blouse and hair all caught in the breeze, Eldie on the dirt road that turns to pavement once the beaches are in view.

You try the number one more time, and your heart sinks at that ring, tinny like a coin clinking against the walls of an empty well. You drop the receiver and hurry to the street. A block down, the clock over the liquor mart reads 6:43. You spit—old lady or no, mud or none, she should have been there to answer.

You walk a ways, grinding your teeth and following your feet past shops displaying knockoff jerseys and shiny white shoes, baseball caps and cowboy hats, wool blankets of brightly colored stripes or La Virgen in her starry blue robe, any number of things to send home: towels, toiletries, batteries, toys, magazines, glow-in-the-dark rosaries, packaged dinners, candy. All the shops and smells and street vendors shouting out frutas y churros y dulces reminds you of the square in Veracruz on a slow day. You walk into the Gato Negro. The bar is dark and filled with the sounds of clicking pool cues and cumbia from an electric jukebox. You find a space at the bar and order a beer, feeling justified: you didn't have to pay for lunch. Somewhere between the dial tone and the front door of the Gato Negro, you decided that you deserve something better than heading back to the garage to wait for tomorrow. You at least deserve a beer today.

Tommy's behind the bar, of course, and on a stool you recognize Jimmy, one of the regulars from the Zone. He invites you to sit with him and the others in the back. Felipe is there, and a few other faces you recognize, gathered around a worn bar table with cigarette packs and beer bottles strewn across it. They are toasting a good day, a profitable day of pouring foundation for a new pet store in Emeryville. "God bless the little dogs and cats and fishes," someone says amid the clinking glasses. You sip your beer, considering how to get closer to Felipe. You want to ask if they're working the same site tomorrow and if they need another man on their crew. But halfway through your beer, you have decided this doesn't sit well with you. It feels like begging.

Besides, an extra man could be a cut in their wages. So you hold your empty beer bottle and laugh at Jimmy's jokes.

Another guy from the Zone, Manny, starts talking about the harvest work up north, how he and his wife and sons had a car and would follow the harvest from Santa Clara to Portland and sometimes up into Washington. The idea of having a car makes your mouth twitch into a smile—all the places you could go. You could drive up to the Sierras and get a job at that resort. You could go somewhere else, someplace new, maybe up north like Manny. There's a lot of work up north, he says, lots of places a man can find a job.

Happy hour is over at eight o'clock, and the beers are back to full price. The men are pulling on their coats and throwing dollars into a loose stack atop the bill. Some are going home to families, to their wives and children. You think of Eldie and hear the shrill ring of the phone, ringing and ringing. The cut on your side flares. You want another beer.

Felipe lingers at the table, and you catch his eye as the others leave. "That wasn't enough for me. Want another round?"

He nods and claps a hand on your shoulder. "I'm glad you have enough sense to want to buy me one more."

At the bar, you put down one of the twenties from your roll, and Tommy pops the caps off two bottles, shoves limes in their spouts. Jukebox country songs, snippets of bar talk—soccer, broads, bosses, football. The noise is a comfort, drowning out the thoughts that would otherwise overwhelm you. Jimmy sticks around too, and you listen to him and Felipe go back and forth about San Jose and the cost of gas and how pretty the wife is back home, wherever home is. For Jimmy, home is down the block from the garage. You realize you don't know where Felipe is from. He's fast at conversation, knows how to blare his voice, yet somehow always avoids the particulars of his own life. All you really know about Felipe is that he can't wait to get to somewhere else.

What was supposed to be one round turns into three. A small mountain of shavings builds as you and Felipe peel the labels off your bottles and shred them to little wisps. Jimmy leaves to settle up at the bar, and Felipe leans toward you secretively. "I'm telling you straight. I got a friend up in Reno who is doing very well. You remember Salvador? He's the one back from L.A. who lugged that TV with him everywhere. He's been working in Reno for the last few months. He's got his own place even."

"What's he doing up that way?"

Felipe slams his bottle down a little too hard. "Condos, casinos...Does it matter? Trust me, he's got better prospects."

In your mind, you see snowy mountains, the sky white and the mountains green with trees. You can barely tolerate a Bay Area winter. "How cold does it get up there?"

Felipe sighs. "Not so bad. All cold is about the same after zero degrees, and then it's just a matter of how strong the wind is."

When the three of you are the only ones not standing at the bar, you all head out of the Gato Negro. You intend to head to the bus stop up the street, but before you get there, Felipe has wandered into a bodega on the corner. As you follow, you intend to go to the back and grab a tall can, but Felipe is in front of the liquor cabinet. He spends eight dollars and forty-seven cents on a small bottle of tequila, the middle-size one that looks the least like piss, and cracks the seal as the electric pulse signals his exit. The air has warmed up with the night, or your body has with the beers. Either way, you decide it's a nice night to walk. It's only a mile and a half back to the garage.

The night is purple, cut with dry orange light beneath the streetlamps. The streets are clear, but not quiet. There are voices everywhere. Murmurs and laughter fall out open windows of passing cars. Subwoofers rumble from blocks away. The street crackles softly beneath your feet.

Jimmy and Felipe walk ahead of you, talking about Reno. Everyone seems to have a friend somewhere. Jimmy knows a guy in Reno too who works the ski lodges. Says he plows snow in the winter and cuts grass in the summer, and has made enough to send for his wife and kids. Now Jimmy's friend has got to figure out what to do with the girl he's seeing in Reno, how to break it off before the real family arrives and their new life begins. "What a good problem to have," Felipe says, his words starting to join together.

Felipe passes the bottle, and you work on it slowly at first, taking small swigs as you make your way down the avenue. You count the streets with sips—Twenty-fifth, Twenty-eighth, Park Street, Thirty-third, Fruitvale Avenue. Before long, your arms and belly are warm with drink, and you pull at the collar of your sweatshirt. The shops have brought in their clothing displays and lowered their shutters. The bottle is half empty, and you are half-way home, which is now the last place you want to be. You are starting to hate the peeling paint on the walls and the rustling draft that gets under the door, and you recognize that familiar feeling about the apartment in Los Angeles and about the trailer in Phoenix, how you begin to hate the place you're supposed to rest your head at night. You pull back the bottle and drink until it burns the back of your throat.

At the intersection of Thirty-eighth and East Fourteenth, you spot the silhouette of a girl leaning on a broken phone booth, tight skirt and heels, straight hair hanging like a curtain. Normally, you'd walk right past her, wouldn't even look at her. But normally, Eldie would have picked up. Normally, you wouldn't be drunk. Normally, you could tolerate the pain in your back from bending and in your feet from standing, and this cut wouldn't be slicing into you with each movement.

"Hungry, fella?" Felipe jabs you, and you realize your pace has slowed. The girl looks away, kicks a leg out. You imagine her smoky lined eyes looking up at you, her ribs rising as she pulls off that pink top, the warm softness centered in that stretch of black skirt. You shake your head and keep walking, but Felipe is on you now, has a new focal point to fixate on. "Go on, man, you can have her."

The bills are in your back pocket. You touch them, the edges soft, almost the same texture as your jeans. You think of the house you worked on today, its swirling Sheetrock white dust, and how nothing seemed to wash away the vague taste of paint in your mouth.

"Hey, lady!" Felipe whistles. The girl looks your way. Something rises up in you, somewhere in your stomach, and you almost turn around to see her. You quicken your pace down the street. "No, compa, come back! She likes you!" he shouts, but you keep moving forward. Damn your eyes, this place. Damn that old woman tying up the line. Damn Eldie for not answering. You'd never have even looked otherwise.

You hear Felipe trotting behind you, half-drunk laughter spilling out of him, and he pushes into your side. Like that, you are on fire, your whole hip a spasm of fresh pain. Wincing, you turn and push, make contact with his chest. He rears back, the pendulum swinging from giddy to belligerent. You read each other, tight arms and balled fists. Suddenly, readily, you hate him, his big mouth always talking and his eyes always looking for a way out of here. He swings at you, and you swing back, and before Jimmy can break the two of you apart, you have both landed blows. You know it's Felipe, and you know he's your friend, but at the same time, you keep throwing out your fists. You don't know what you're punching at.

Jimmy presses Felipe against the wall of a building, and with nowhere to direct your weight, you stumble to the ground. The effort to look at it is tremendous, this dark stain growing on your jeans. Blood pools hot on your side, the tape dislodged, the scab broken.

Felipe curses you from the wall, and Jimmy holds him by the shoulders. You curse them both, pull yourself off the curb, and stumble down the street. Stumbling turns to running, but running like a child—your whole body leaning forward, your momentum carrying you more than your feet or your will over them. By the time you stop and turn, you are alone, no sign of Felipe. Hopefully Jimmy took him to his house and put him on the couch to sleep it off. Maybe you'll get the bed to yourself tonight. You can bleed all over it in peace. No more talk of mountains, no more snow. Rounding the corner into the residentials, chest burning, mouth dry, you know you're going to vomit, it's just a matter of when.

The walk back to the garage is only a few blocks, but all the streets roll out in front of you like endless paths, variable end points from here, variable destinations. Some come to the states and send money home once a week. Some come to the states, send money back for a while, then disappear, their lives enveloped in new possibilities, American opportunities. Some travel to new cities every few weeks, a new place to go to before the one you're in gets to you too much. They leave wives, sons and daughters, sick mothers and disappointed fathers beyond a border drawn on a map, a line that's only imaginary until they have crossed it. You think how simple it would be to find a truck heading for some job out of state, work for yourself and no one else. No more money going back home, no more beans and coffee but steak and eggs every morning. And then you think of Eldie, think of her in your father's kitchen with planks for a floor, and your stomach lurches as the thought of leaving her for good fully forms.

The house you stay in is just down the street, but you duck into the graveled space between two houses and rest your hands on your knees. Your whole body aches, the pain branching out from the cut on your hip, or maybe some other place, and you wonder if you're finally going to wretch or if this heave will pass and leave you be. Your mouth is mealy, your fingers fat with salt and blood. You fall into a squat, then finally sprawl out on the bed of rocks. The sky is a blanket over you. Bills from your roll have flown out of your hands and are out in the world. They will not go to Poza Rica. They will stay here in Oakland. Those bills will work their way through other hands in this city, spread out thin across many places, and maybe, if you're lucky, they might return to you, almost in one piece.

LITTERS

N OT MANY TRAVELED the dirt road that wound off Del Puerto Canyon in Patterson; it led nowhere but the Marino house, and the Marinos rarely had visitors. Should someone happen up the road, after a mile or two of rolling brown hills, a muffled, indistinct chorus of barks would echo in greeting from somewhere between the hills and the interstate a few miles beyond. A high-pitched yelp or howl would catch the driver's ear, make them jump and their eyes swivel off the gravel road, looking for its source. Della Marino had seen this reaction when she was younger, when she'd been driven home by her friends' mothers after a slumber party or a softball practice. The barking registered in Della's ears over the engine and the gravel hitting the undercarriage, but with years of practice, she had made an art of ignoring the howls that came from the cellar of her house.

The two-story farmhouse had once been yellow, but the paint had faded to a dingy gray. Della parked in the shade cast from the pitched roof, and she stepped over Pancha on the front porch, minding the splay of the dog's shriveled back legs. The toy terrier made a noise somewhere between a growl and a moan, and Della returned Pancha's glare as she slipped through the front door.

Walking in, she dropped her keys in the candy dish filled with coins and laid her red jacket (the gold lapel emblem indicating her junior status, qualified to tour lots and set up refinance meetings) on the coat rack. The midafternoon light poured through the kitchen windows and spilled in straight columns down the hallway. She could hear her mother's afternoon pot of coffee percolating.

In the kitchen, Della found her mother in her usual place at the counter, her mug in one hand, while the other worked the grip of the crutch holding her up.

"The doctor said to stay off your feet. Sit down," Della said, studying the cast encasing her mother's right leg from ankle to thigh. It made her look more willowy than she was—her thin frame hid muscle. Rhoda worked herself straight, adjusting the crutch under her arm.

"How was work?" she asked, stirring sugar in her cup.

Della sat at the kitchen table and adjusted her chair so she wasn't looking straight at the cellar door. "Some developer finally bought the Petersen lot."

"More condos." Rhoda smirked—Della could hear it in her voice. The suburban tracts had been inching up the brown hills surrounding their land for years. Most of the other farming families had traded their dry acreage for an address on one of the newly paved Patterson streets, but Rhoda steadfastly refused to sell. Her mother would never part from this stretch, no matter how much money they could get for it. The daily average price index for Stanislaus County acreage scrolled across Della's computer screen at work every few minutes, and sometimes—for fun—she would multiply the value by fifty-two to see what Rhoda could cash out with on the land alone.

"You work on Saturday?" Rhoda huffed and turned toward her daughter.

"No." Della reached for the newspaper and scanned the head-lines. The kitchen smelled like coffee and bananas about to turn from resting in the sun.

"Good. I'll need you to take a few out to Oakland."

Della dropped the paper. "I thought I was going up Monday." She was afraid her voice sounded like a whine. When Rhoda had fractured her leg two months before, it had fallen on Della to drive to the Bay Area and drop off the pups to the buyers. Rhoda had handled all aspects of the business after Della's father, Tony, had died, from breeding and weaning the pups to taking them out to buyers. Since Della had graduated from high school last year, Rhoda expected her to be more involved with the business. It was easier when Della was young, when she thought all the dogs they bred in the cellar were destined for families and green backyards. Now Della had to take the pups out of the pens her-self and deliver them to whatever fate the buyer had in mind. The prospect of driving another batch out made her feel like her mouth was full of sand, each dry grain scratching down her throat. "Just let me take care of it all in one day."

"Mr. Robson needs them on Saturday, not Monday."

"Can't he come out here?" Della muttered.

Rhoda's eyes sharpened onto her daughter. "You got some-thing more important to do?" Her voice strengthened without rising in pitch.

Della roughly shook out a crease in the paper fold. "Fine. I'll leave tomorrow at ten." She winced at her own voice, a nasally whine when she was angry, and wished she had one as thick and strong as Rhoda's.

"It won't take you but the morning." Rhoda's rigid stance didn't ease as she took up her mug. The only sounds came from the rustle of the trees outside and the occasional whimper from the cellar a few feet away.

"While you're out that way, may as well take Jake's things to him before he goes to Cleveland," Rhoda said. She hadn't said anything about Jake in weeks. Della didn't want to meet her mother's eyes, the cool blue stare that sometimes looked like rocks, or the sky, things hard or far away. "That way you won't have to make any extra trips."

Della wanted to say, "You're heartless," felt the words forming in her mouth, but she couldn't muster anything more than to shake the paper, draw it taut in front of her face so her mother wouldn't see her seething.

THAT SATURDAY DELLA found everything she needed for the drive to Oakland right by the front door: thirty-five dollars for gas, two grocery bags full of Jake's clothes, and three pit bull pups asleep in a mesh-wire cage. A cardboard box sat next to the door with a cotton shirt at the bottom. Rhoda had set up the pups for her to take, and Della was glad of it. She hated going into the cellar, where the pups and bitches were kept in separate rooms. No matter the time of year, the cellar was always colder than the rest of the house; Della's teeth chattered whenever she put kibble in bowls or lined the pens with blankets and towels—an involuntary response to the chill. When she collected the pups for delivery, her fingers would ache with cold in the soft fold of puppy fur, gooseflesh signaling up and down her skin. Grabbing a pup from its litter, the others bit at her sleeves, and the bitch bleated jagged barks from her crate. Every time, they howled and cried, as if they knew where those pups were going.

The little things struggled, whined, resisted as much as they could as Della plucked each one from the cage by the scruff of its neck and placed it in the box. She took the pups to the car last, after Jake's things and her CDs for the hour-and-a-half drive. Rhoda was up and moving somewhere in the house, but Della didn't seek her out to say good-bye.

The cardboard box kept shifting on the way out of Patterson, and Della steadied it when she heard too much shuffling or a yelp from sharp teeth against a neck or an ear. One hand on the box, the other on the steering wheel, she thought how her cousin Jake would have the pups settled and asleep before they had left the valley.

Jake had come to live with Rhoda and Della that past Christmas. Though he was five years younger, Jake and Della always played together during holidays and barbecues, when he and his mother Lucinda drove out to Patterson. The two chased the pups around the yard while Lucinda sat with Rhoda under the hickory tree, and the two women talked about Tony with moist eyes and warm beers in hand. Lucinda died quietly in her sleep that past November—the tumor in her right breast and the lesions along her liver were discovered postmortem. Rhoda was the closest kin that Jake had in the state, as his own father had been gone since he was a toddler. Jake came to live on the ranch eighty miles away from the only home he'd ever known in Palo Alto.

Once Jake was at the ranch, he immersed himself in the dogs. He fed the pups and ran the mothers and studs out in the field, and attended to the tasks that Della had always complained about. Jake's clutter turned the still house into an obstacle course: the pups chewed on his high-tops and dragged his dirty socks through the yard by their teeth. His basketball was always rolling off the porch and down the driveway. Della enjoyed swerving to miss it when she arrived home from work at night.

But on the April night that Rhoda fell down the stairs and broke her leg, Jake disappeared out of the house. Della had gone out that night and come home to the front door swinging open: she found Rhoda at the bottom of the stairs and took her to the hospital, then returned to the ranch to look for Jake. Driving through the black night over dirt roads, Della's eyes hurt from staring through the dusty windshield, hoping to see the flash of Jake's body in the glow of the headlights. Her knuckles were white mountains plastered to the steering wheel. When Rhoda came home the next morning, she didn't say what had set Jake off, but insisted he'd be back. Two days later, a South Bay officer found Jake riding a bus in Tracy, looking for the transfer route to Palo Alto. Not long after that, a social worker decided other arrangements were to be made for Jake's care, and he was sent to a foster home in the Oakland hills.

The pups were beginning to doze as Della exited the freeway and traversed Ninety-eighth Avenue. She eyed the liquor marts and cheap clothing stores, the gas stations and fish fry joints lined up like a long trail of matchbooks on their sides. Old men stood in the doorways of their shops, drinking from Styrofoam cups. People waiting for buses adjusted their coats and looked to the sky, hedging their bets between when the rain would start and when the bus would arrive. Della made her way off Ninety-eighth into a maze of back streets and potholed alleys, over speed bumps ten feet across. She knew how to get to Robson's place by feel more than by street. She remembered driving there with her parents, and they all grilled steaks and Della played with Robson's daughters. He was her Uncle Robson, who gave her candy when he visited the ranch. After Tony died, Rhoda took her to Robson's to drop off the pups, but there were no barbecues, no other kids to play with. Della followed the brick retaining wall for several blocks to Robson's place at the very end of the dead-end street.

Robson was waiting for her, watering bright pink and white flowers in clay pots that lined the wooden fence separating the house from the kennels in the backyard. He was in his sixties, but he was tall and sturdy, his thick build hidden under a black raincoat. Della pulled into the graveled driveway and stopped just short of Robson's feet. She gave him a hug after climbing out of the car. Robson finished his watering. They talked about the drive, about the bad weather. The dark clouds stretching over the bay showed no signs of breaking.

Robson turned to the box in the car. "They done weaning yet?"

Della didn't like the question. It meant the pups were too small. "They've been on solids for over a week." She opened the passenger door, grabbed the box, and put it on the ground. Robson grabbed one of the pups by the scruff of its neck, held it midair in one hand as he felt along the dog's rib cage and hips with the other. His hands were callused, but careful, inspecting. Della thought of her father, who had smooth, hard palms and black hairs on his knuckles.

"Pretty scrawny for seven weeks. I could crush this pup in my hand."

"Well, shoot, Mr. Robson. You got some big hands." Della tried to smile like all of this was harmless. Robson turned the pup over, considering it, then dropped it nonchalantly back with the other two. "Your mom said she had rotts for me this time."

If Rhoda were here, she would have cut him down, told him

she knew what he wanted better than he did, so take the damn dogs and be happy about it. "The pits are in better shape. She said you'd like these better."

"Is that what she said," he murmured, a smile forming and then falling from his face. He pulled a roll from his jacket pocket and peeled six hundred dollar bills. "Them two will do. That red one's of no use to me." Della slipped the warm bills into her front pocket. The pups squirmed atop one another in the box. Robson pulled a cigar from behind his ear, lit it, and chomped on the plastic tip. "How's your mom these days?" He exhaled smoke and adjusted his body against the fence.

"She's getting better. Should be back on her feet by the end of the month." Della absently kicked at the gravel. "She's got mainly pits and rotts right now, a few Dobies. Lots of folks want pits or rotts. I gotta come up about once a week."

"She still bringing up them terriers, too?" Robson drew on the cigar slowly. She watched the yellow-gray smoke swirl in his mouth.

"None of them for more than a year. After the whole flap with that bad crossbreed, she don't like working the fads no more." They had stopped breeding toy dogs after a girl from Blackhawk bought a terrier that developed a bad case of hip dysplasia. The girl threatened to call animal control when Rhoda couldn't produce the health certificates for the dog. It was too close for Rhoda's taste. By then, most of the dogs had doctored papers or weren't on record at all. She gave the girl a refund and took the twisted dog, little Pancha, who followed Della around the house, grunting from the work of dragging her back legs behind her.

A pup yelped from the box. Robson kicked the side, denting

the cardboard. Della turned away, looked at the tufts of weeds and grass and the empty metal cages, at the sun-bleached planks of the wooden fence.

"I should get going. I don't want to hit traffic out of town," Della said, checking her watch, even though she knew the time. Robson grabbed the two pups and put them in metal crates against the fence. He turned, dug into another pocket, and fished out a smaller roll. He unfurled a twenty and put it in her hand.

"Stop by Little Peking and get some lunch," he said, and gave her a kiss on the cheek. "Tell Miss Rhoda I'll be talking to her."

Robson took one of the crates toward the kennels as she backed out of the driveway. One of the pups was solid black, the other, brown with white spots spread across its back. The lonely pup whined in the box, brownish red with a perfect white circle over its left eye. It had weak hips and legs: she could tell by the angle of the feet, the protrusion of the pelvis. No good for guarding or fighting. Tony never would have sold Robson a dog like that. The dogs that came from their stock could hold up at any pedigree show. Everything changed when Della was eight, when Tony tried to break up a bar fight between two strangers; he stepped between two Fresno bikers and got a bar stool slammed against the base of his skull.

Robson disappeared around the bend, the crate in hand, and Della felt her jaw aching from clenched teeth. She gripped the twenty tight and pulled back onto the street.

DELLA STRETCHED IN the front seat and studied the contrast of gray sky kissing gray ocean. The sky had texture and volume with its clouds billowing under and atop one another, while the ocean remained strangely calm, a motionless shine that tapered into darkness at the far corners of Della's sight. The marina was deserted save a few joggers and a pair on a bench sharing a paper-bagged drink. Della watched them intently, trying not to focus on the scents of piss and puppy fur that now pervaded the sedan. The bills in her pocket itched against her thigh.

The pup startled her with a yowl from the backseat, and Della tossed a bit of chicken from her white takeout box. It chewed loudly and whined again. After a moment, she wrestled the cardboard into the front and rubbed the pup's neck. "Come on now. Hush up," Della cooed, reaching into the box to pet the little thing into silence. The pup stretched out on its back, its belly pink and round under Della's palm. She suddenly remembered being a little girl in her backyard when her parents built the first kennels—under a lemony sun, Della stroked the soft belly of a pup in her lap and listened to her parents laugh as they built another kennel out of plywood and chicken wire.

Rhoda and Tony had bred dogs before Della was born: one of Tony's coworkers at the milk plant had a Doberman bitch in heat, and Tony had a Dobie named Roscoe with papers. They began studding Roscoe out, and they kept one of the bitches from a litter that had good stock on both sides. First they bred Dobies, then Weimaraners and retrievers and Dalmatians, large breeds that they sold to families. But then Tony had his accident, as the family called it. When they went to the hospital, Della looked at her father, his head wrapped in bandages, and could see only the swollen skin around his neck. It looked like a pregnant bitch's stomach, stretched and bloated, teeming with something that needed to be expelled. He was in the hospital for seventeen days, then the doctors turned off the respirator.

Time divided evenly around that day for Della, like the divide between night and day. Her father was there, then he was gone. Everything around the ranch suddenly seemed drained: the dogs were listless, the wind struggled against perpetual clouds, the rain stirred a metallic smell in the air. Even the dust was a gray ash that worked its way under windowpanes and through crevices in the walls, collecting at the roof of the mouth and the corners of the eyes. Rhoda spent the weeks after Tony died moving everything out of the cellar and setting up the kennels and crates. All the mothers went from the backyard into the cellar, and the pups were taken in and put in wooden pens. Outside, the wood beams of the kennels warped in the rain; the cage door hinges rusted shut.

Della's phone rang as the pup jumped toward a piece of chicken dangling from her fingers.

"So did he take them?"

"He took two of them. I don't think he was happy about it." Della popped a red pepper into her mouth. "Said he wanted rotts, not pits."

"Well, he can get to liking it. He ain't aiming for quality," Rhoda said. "When are you getting back?"

"I'm going to that group home. I want to see Jake since I'm here." Rhoda didn't respond. Della was used to this kind of silence. "I figured I'd take him for ice cream or something," she said as she flicked a grain of rice off her shirt.

"Try to be back at six. It's a trick to feed all of them with this thing on my leg," Rhoda said, and the phone clicked silent.

Della dropped the phone in her lap and rolled her neck. She dug in her purse and looked through a small notepad filled with phone numbers, directions, lists of groceries or errands with lines drawn through them. In the middle of the notebook, sandwiched between directions to a client's house in Vallejo and a blue ink sketch of a polar bear was the number for the group home Jake lived in.

"Enrichment House. Can I help you?" Della recognized the voice of Janet, one of the staff. She had never spoken with her, only heard Janet's voice on her message service after coming unannounced to the group home when Jake was first placed there. The message was brief, and Janet crisply insisted that one must call ahead before visiting.

"This is Della Marino, Jake Marino's cousin. I was hoping I could come see Jake today," Della said. She felt put on the spot, like she should have an official reason for seeing the boy.

"Jake has an appointment in an hour or so, and he'll be available around seven o'clock tonight," Janet said, her voice softer than Della recalled.

"Well...how about I come and see him right now? I can be there in fifteen minutes." Della straightened up in her seat and started the ignition.

"I'll tell him you're on your way."

JAKE ANSWERED THE door when Della rang the doorbell. His smile showed new braces with neon-yellow bands. He walked her into the house. The walls were whitewashed, and the front room was bare save for several mismatched leather couches and a wooden clock on the wall with a picture of Jesus lacquered under the dial hands. Janet sat in a folding chair in the archway; she shook Della's hand, had her sign her name in a guest registry, and told her to have Jake back by two o'clock.

In two months, Jake's legs and his thick brown hair had sprouted two inches. As he carried the grocery bags filled with his clothes from the ranch down the hallway, Della wondered if they would fit him anymore. He was almost as tall as her now, especially with that puff of hair on his head. They had the same kind of hair—thick and unruly, dark brown with an auburn sheen. Walking out to the sedan, she pointed to the pup in the back of the car. He studied it through the glass and asked if she had a leash. "Let's take him for a walk," he said, tapping his fingers against the window.

She didn't have a leash, but she found a length of rope in the trunk. Jake fashioned a small knot and maneuvered the rope gently around the pup's neck. Jake set the pup down, and it immediately barreled down the street, choking itself with every leap forward. After five blocks, Jake carried the pup in his arms, laughed as it nestled into the fold of his coat. They talked about the puppy, his new school, and the things he was and wasn't learning in his eighth-grade class. They splashed through the puddles from yesterday's rain, the cuffs of their jeans wet against their ankles.

Circling the neighborhood, they wandered the sloping streets until they came to an elementary school playground, and they settled on a bench near the gate. The clouds were patching as they usually did at midday, revealing holes of bright blue sky. Jake set the pup at his feet, where it plopped and chewed on the dewy grass.

"So Nona called last week," Della said after a while. "She said you're going to stay with her for a while."

Jake watched the pup at his feet. "Yeah. That's going to be weird," he muttered. He leaned down and pulled at a few blades of grass. "You ever been to Cleveland? This guy who lives with me says it snows there all the time."

"Maybe it snows in the winter, but I bet it's nice the rest of the year. Every place has some kind of summer," Della said. "Nona said she's got a room all set up for you." The last time Della had seen her grandmother was at Lucinda's funeral. She flew in from Cleveland and stayed in the ranch house cooking. Nona acted the same way when Tony died: nothing could get her out of that kitchen. She cooked all kinds of Sicilian foods and sang songs that Della remembered her father singing while playing with the dogs. The smell of garlic and marinara could still jolt her back to those funerary days of Nona dropping chunks of white fish into a vat of tomatoes, a streak of flour under her eye where she wiped away tears. Jake nodded but said nothing.

"I wish things had worked better at the ranch. I liked having you there with us. Aunt Rhoda too," Della said, keeping her eyes on her boots.

Jake shifted in his seat. "You sure?"

Della pushed a nervous laugh out of her chest. "Of course. Your auntie never cooked until you came around. And she never let me play with the pups in the house."

Jake shrugged. "I liked it out there. It was better than the group home."

Della realized there was no better time to ask than now. "So what happened? That night?"

"I don't know, it's hard to—" Jake's voice sputtered. He leaned over again, plucked at the same spot of grass. He was quiet for a while, his fingers working the grass blades into twisted ropes. "You remember the rott that was about to have her puppies?"

Which one? Which time? Della thought at first, but then she remembered that night in April, the rott laboring. Rhoda was sure it would be an easy birth, but she wanted Della to stay and help. Della had refused: she could spend her night covered in blood in the cellar, or she could drink iced coffee with her girlfriends from the office. The choice seemed simple; the consequences limited.

Jake tucked his chin between his knees and tugged lightly on the pup's rope leash. "Auntie told me to stay out of there. She said I shouldn't watch, that it was messy and I didn't need to see it. I listened at the door, you know, and after the pups were all born, Auntie came up. She was busy doing something in the kitchen, and I wanted to go look, you know? I just wanted to see the pups all brand new." Jake paused.

"Did you go down there?" Della felt something coiling itself tight in her chest.

"I just went down there to look real quick. I saw the mama dog lying out, and all her pups were squirming and moving around. They were hairless and wet and weird looking, but still cute. I was just looking at them for a minute. And then the mama dog started freaking out and sniffing at the pups and barking. And I called your mom, but she didn't come. And she started moving around all funny, and I yelled, 'She's doing something!' And then the mama dog turned and just bit into one of them pups, hard.

"I didn't know what to do. I tried to grab the baby from the mama, but she just kept holding it and jerked it out of my hands. Chomped on my finger. I couldn't do nothing—" Jake's eyes barreled down on the horizon, still gray and dark with clouds.

"The dog just ate it, ate the baby. Your mom came running down, and she fell off that loose middle step, and she started crying when she landed on the floor. She kept saying to me, 'Get

out, Jake. Don't look.' I saw all that blood, and Auntie was crying and yelling at me, and all the dogs were barking, it was—"

Della rubbed the space between his bony shoulder blades.
She had seen the same thing when she was a kid. It was nighttime, and she could hear her parents helping a Dobie give birth
in the cellar; she peered through the cracked door, trying to see.
Rhoda held one of the pups, and Tony had hunched over the
wooden pen, his arms held out in the air, the mother snapping
at him. When Della saw the blood on his hands, she thought the
mama dog had bitten him. The naked lightbulb swung back and
forth over their heads, as if pushed by the voices and barking in
the room. She could hear the gnarled sound of chewing from
the stairs, and when her father moved, she saw the dog's jaws
snapping into a red mess. Della didn't remember crying, but she
must have because her next memory is Tony reaching for her on
the steps, his hands slick with blood and afterbirth, his bony
cheek pressed hard against her own.

"I saw that, too, when I was maybe six. Scared the shit outta
me." Della laughed nervously. "I wanted to see, too, and I didn't
know what was happening. I just saw all this blood, and my dad
came up to me, set me at the kitchen table. He said after the
mama dog has all her pups, she gets real hungry, and she needs
to eat. And sometimes, when she doesn't get something to eat
real quick, she'll have to take one of the pups back in so she
can make milk and feed her other babies. That's how dad said
it—she just takes it back in. She doesn't know that we have food
for her. It doesn't make sense to us, and it doesn't make sense to
the mama dog, but she has to do it. She has to do it because she
loves her babies so much…"

She stopped short at her father's words coming out of her

mouth. Della turned and studied her cousin: his face was starting to change, his once chubby cheeks hardening. She wondered if her face had changed when her father died, if her eyes had set as deeply as Jake's had since he lost his mother. "I'm sorry I wasn't there that night. I should have been there."

"How could you know?" Jake said. The pup began chewing on the orange nylon rope. "I just wanted to go back home, back to where I lived with my mom. I miss her."

There were no adequate words, so Della rubbed his back some more, trying to let him know through her touch that it was all right, that some things need no apology, and that there are some things an apology can never truly mend.

"She ate it 'cause she was hungry?" Jake asked, not looking up.

"She had to feed her other pups," Della whispered. "Instinct. It was the only thing she knew to do."

They were quiet a long time, each pair of eyes traveling between the pup, the grass, the dew on their shoes, each other, the sun pushing through and then hiding behind the clouds. Jake pulled the puppy from the ground to his lap. It wrapped its little forelegs around Jake's hand and began mouthing his fingers.

"He likes you," Della said.

The boy smirked and stroked the pup's back. "They like everyone."

IT TOOK ALMOST three hours to get back to Patterson from Oakland—a big rig jackknifed across three lanes on the Altamont pass. After ten minutes of idling, Della shut off the ignition and let the pup out of the box, watching him explore the front seat with timid sniffs and a bark every now and then. Soon the pup curled in her lap and went to sleep. She rubbed its ear between her fingers. If her mother saw this, she would scold her—"Stop treating it like a pet, Dell." The pup didn't wake until the traffic crept forward and Della had to move to shift gears.

"Thank your lucky stars for them bony hips." Della gingerly placed the pup back into the box. The pup sighed and rolled onto his back, licking his muzzle before continuing his interrupted nap.

The traffic started and stopped, slithered its way down the interstate. The morning cloud cover was long gone in the valley, and the heat shimmered across the streets of Patterson like oil smoking on a warm skillet. As always, Della dropped her keys in the coin bowl and her bag on the armchair, managing to keep the puppy propped against her shoulder. Della almost didn't see Rhoda in the living room—they rarely used the room except to walk through it.

"How was the drive?" her mother spoke from behind a piece of paper. She sat on the corner of the sofa with bills and envelopes scattered around her, her cast propped up on the coffee table. Pancha was at her feet, her tongue out and back legs sprawling.

"Fine. It wasn't too hot on the road."

Rhoda finally looked up. "That's the one he didn't want?" Della didn't answer and adjusted the writhing dog in her arms.

"Take it down and put it in the top row." Rhoda dropped a paper in a pile and moved on to another envelope.

"Its hips are bad, you know," Della murmured.

Rhoda chuckled and shook her head. "Take it downstairs."

She scribbled loud enough for Della to hear the pen scratch across the paper. The pup squirmed in her arms, and as she moved through the hallway toward the kitchen, her grip tightened around the little rib cage in her hands. The cellar door was ajar, a cool darkness floating up the stairs.

Della dropped the pup and marched back to the living room, her face hot, her hands forming fists. "Aren't you going to ask about him?"

Rhoda didn't look up. "What's to ask? Everything's all worked out. He'll go to Cleveland. Nothing to talk about." Her voice was thin and high, as if she were commenting on the weather or the deer that graze in the hills.

"Mom, Jake told me about that night. You said he just took off. You could've explained it. He could have come back—"

"You must've left your brain in the bay, Dell. You think I'm going to have some social worker poking around our house, in the cellar?" Rhoda's voice was granite. The paper in her hand tented around the pressure of her grip.

"So you let him run? You just let him go like that?"

"The state sent him to me, and now they're going to find something else for him. I did the best I could. That's all I ever can do." Rhoda's eyes seemed to drill into the page she held. "It's too bad it happened that way, but it's out of my hands."

Della felt a rush of heat course through her. "That's not right, Mom. Jake wasn't some dog you could just pass off—"

"I won't have a little girl tell me what's what." Rhoda finally looked up from the bill in her hand. "I took that boy in and I wanted him here, but once he took off like that, it was out of my hands. I'm not having anyone come to my house to see how my life is run." Rhoda's voice never wavered with emotion, only flattened. "You do what you have to, Dell. Everything starts to fall down if you start looking beyond your own."

Della shook her head. "He's ours. He's blood, and you let him go. Dad never would have let things turn out like this."

"Don't talk to me about what he would or wouldn't have done. Your daddy would have done anything to make sure you have a future," Rhoda snapped back. She stared at her daughter as her finger dug under the flap of an envelope, ripping it open. "You're spoiled. You don't know a damn thing."

Sweat beaded Della's forehead, but her hands felt clammy, like she was holding ice. "When that cast comes off, I'm not doing any more deliveries for you. I won't do anything to help you with the dogs anymore." The words were jagged in her throat. Everything about her felt raw, like she had ripped away an old scab and found blood brimming. She turned and strode toward the kitchen door, the pup stumbling underfoot. "And when you die, I'm selling this place," Della said over her shoulder. Rhoda shouted something as the door slammed behind her, but Della didn't stop. Ignoring the itch of tears in her eyes, she paced to the cages, every part of her body wiry and tight. She trained her gaze on the bend of highway that could be seen between the hills. She let her vision blur until the parallel streams of red brake lights and white headlamps were swaths of light working their backs against each other, touching on their separate ways to north and south.

The kitchen door clapped shut, and Della expected to see her mother hobbling over. But instead, Pancha had squirmed through the door, working her front legs hard down the porch steps. The pup trotted up to sniff at Pancha's warped rear end, and the two reared and pounced. The pup fell under its clumsy legs and rolled on its back as Pancha chewed on his neck. The crippled dog jumped and cowed the pup, his hips and legs caked with red dust.

Better use those legs while you can, Della thought, waiting for the pup to squirm off his back and run.

MASHA'ALLAH

I T WILL PROBABLY snow on the pass to Reno, Sullivan Gibbs
thinks as he pulls the black Lincoln town car against the curb.
If he and Suze and Cherise leave tomorrow night, maybe they'll
miss the storm, let it pass them, and they'll be in the casinos after
the storm has cleared. Suze is probably packing her casino-wear
right now, and he imagines his wife in her gold and black lamé
smock, shimmering tights, and her silver slippers, the lucky flats
she always wears when they go to San Pablo or Reno or any of
the Indian casinos between. "Silver and gold, Sully baby," she
will coo at him on the drive through the Sierras, fluffing her dyed-
black hair every now and then. When they were first married, she
would prop her right foot (sans silver shoe) in the crook of the
passenger side mirror and lay her long arm along the ridge of the
seat, her fingers grazing the hair on his neck. He wants to turn to
the empty passenger seat as a reflex, as if to catch a glimpse of
the twenty-three-year-old Suze reclining across the black leather.
Of course she isn't there, and she isn't twenty-three anymore. He
laughs a little at that, how far he and Suze are from twenty-three,
and how they are only getting farther away.

The rain drives hard against the townie's windows, slithering
down the waxed exterior. Mr. Edward's flight is at 2:20 in the
afternoon, and Sully has the executive at San Francisco Interna-

tional Airport at 12:55, allowing a healthy amount of time for check-in and security. Sully opens the back door with one hand and holds an umbrella out with the other to shield his passenger.

"Enjoy Cincinnati, sir," Sully says as Mr. Edwards takes his briefcase and then the umbrella from Sully, lifts himself from the seat, and strides toward the sliding glass doors without a word. Sully waits a beat until his regular is inside and then quickly jumps back into the townie, dusting away the water beads from his cap and wool coat. Pulling off his cap and looking in the rearview, his cheeks are ruddy, and the wet has made his gray temples black again. This is what he needs to stay young, he thinks: a fine, perpetual mist. While the clouds are patching across the bay, the rain hasn't let up over the city, and the wind bites cold.

The cell phone beeps beside him. Cherise. He checks his watch and answers.

"Salaam alaikum, Uncle Sully! Keef halak?" His niece's voice bubbles like Alka-Seltzer. Sully never quite knows how to respond to her Arabic. He feels like he should try to answer her like she wants to be answered, but he always trips over the syllables, mangles the words. So he keeps it simple.

"I'm all right, sweetie. What's going on?"

"Nothing, I'm done with class, and I'm getting on BART. I can't wait for Reno!" He pictures her on the train platform in West Oakland, her backpack slung low on one shoulder and her silver-hooped ear pressed into the phone, how the rain is letting up on that side of the bay, and she can probably see the sun over the water, feel a breath of warmth. "I wanted to ask you, though…" Cherise's voice curls into a question. "Is it okay if Mouhamad comes to dinner tomorrow night, before we leave?"

Sully grimaces. One hungry eighteen-year-old in the house is enough, and the last thing he needs is a hungry boyfriend coming around. Another person at his dinner table chattering in a language he doesn't know. "All right." He nods a little. "But he's not staying too long—"

"Tayeb, tayeb, I know," Cherise says. Sully thinks this must be the tone that parents complain about. She says good-bye in Arabic, and Sully says good-bye in English.

Sully rolls down the window and pulls a pack of Parliaments from the glove box and lights the last white stick in the pack. He's not supposed to smoke in the townie, as per the new company policy. The management firm that took over the car service a few months ago has been getting on all the drivers, especially the ones nearing retirement like Sully, about what they call "professionalism," as in the new black suit policy for drivers and annotating the logs for time spent between pickups. Sully and the other drivers have been doing their best to comply without really complying. On top of that, his next pickup, Mr. Ferdinand, has a notoriously sensitive nose: if he detects smoke or food smells or even a heavy air freshener, he starts sneezing and sniffling and sniveling about his hyperallergenic bronchial-esophageal tract. But Sully doesn't have to pick up Mr. Ferdinand until 3:30 p.m. at the Hilton on Embarcadero, leaving plenty of air-out time. So Sully smokes, sometimes blowing out the window, other times letting the blue smoke drift up against the windshield, its trails straight and undisturbed.

A little farther down the terminal, about a hundred yards away, a fresh batch of arrivals streams out of the glass doors. They look for awnings or run for the parking lot, bending their heads against the rain, with their luggage dawdling behind them. Sully looks at the clock, considers the time. He could pick up a fare easy, maybe even two if the traffic isn't too bad. Sometimes he trolls for cash fares, even though the yellow cabbies give him shit and threaten to call the airport cops when they see his townie in the cab pickup line. He's a poacher, sure, but in the end, catching fares is all about right place and right time—at some point every driver has swooped in to scoop a fare from some other cabbie who wasn't willing to cut a red light or hit the gas a little. It beats heading back to the garage on Harrison Street and sleeping with his cap pulled over his eyes like the other old-timers, riding out the afternoon shifts until they retire. Besides, he could use the extra cash, what with Cherise in the house and the trip to Reno. He always gives Suze the money from picking up fares, and he loves the look on her face when she finds the money tucked in her purse and asks him, "What poor bastard did you shake down so I could have a good time?" She takes care of the bills, never knows how Sully drums up the extra cash, and he likes it that way—Sully can kiss her forehead and never answer her, just do his best Don Corleone as they head into the casino.

The townie creeps at an easy fifteen along the arrival terminals, staying away from the intersections where airport cops stand around and the security level alerts are on display. Sully chucks the last of his cigarette into the falling rain. He looks for the arrivals that scream "business class" with their roll-away leather luggage and matching computer satchels. The ones with rumpled suits are the most likely to jump into the cab and bark a destination, and they're the least likely to ask why Sully doesn't have a meter or his license laminated and taped to the back window. They seem to prefer the townie—they will walk past the yellow cabs with their burgundy velour seats pocked with cigarette burns and make for Sully, just beyond the baggage terminal.

Usually it's quick and clean. He gets the fare to the destination, gets his flat rate of forty dollars and sometimes a tip, and he's back in the city with time to spare in picking up Mr. So-and-So or Ms. Blah Blah Blah. On top of all that, the Associates of Hedrick, Polk, and Lardner catch the cost of gas.

On his third pass around the arrival terminals, Sully spots a woman holding a newspaper over her head at the far end of the American Airlines baggage claim. She's been there on each pass, almost ten minutes, and her coat is soaked through. Tucked beneath a sliver of concrete beside the sliding doors, the wind drives the rain at her. The wipers barely clear the windshield before it blurs with rain again. Normally Sully would pass up a fare like her—he sticks with the suits, always has. He can see one farther down the terminal with just a briefcase and an open umbrella. But the rain is coming down hard, and he decides he'll pick her up; all she has is a newspaper that's warping in her hands. The townie sloshes up to the curb, and it's then that he sees her pregnant belly, which is pulling her closed coat tight around her. Her pink sweater peeks out in little triangle openings between each stressed button. Sully tries to remember the last time he saw a woman that pregnant at the airport. They're few and far between, he's sure of that.

Sully stops, pops the trunk, taps his black hat over his thinning hair, and rolls down the window. "Need a ride, miss?"

The woman looks at Sully from under her sopping newspaper but says nothing. He gets out of the car and walks over, his steps avoiding the rain that runs quick through the gutter. He motions to the suitcase at her feet. "Can I take that?"

After a beat of silence, she steps toward the townie. Sully opens the rear door and gives his most courteous smile. She twists her torso as she gets in, pulling her body in first and her belly in last. Sully picks up the suitcase, which is much heavier than it looked at her feet, pitches it in the trunk, and shuffles around the car into the driver's seat.

"Do you know how to get to the Skyline?" the woman asks in a throaty voice. Sully adjusts the rearview, taking a quick look at the fare. The woman rakes a wet lock of brown hair across her forehead. Her diamond earrings glimmer like the raindrops stuck on the windows. Her tan handbag matches her tan heels. Everything about her looks expensive.

"Off Redwood Road in the hills?" Sully and his friends used to drag their Fords on Redwood and Skyline when they were kids. They'd race up and down the road, dark with tall pines. Those country club pricks at the Skyline always called the cops on them before they could make any juicy bets or settle some real scores.

She looks directly at him in the rearview mirror. "Of course."

He feels a tiny twitch above his eyebrow press and then release. "Sixty dollars," Sully says and pulls away from the curb. He wonders why this woman doesn't have a ride. She looks like the type who would have a car service at her beck and call, or some eager husband to pick her up at the very least. But he dismisses the thought. *You never can tell,* he thinks, and merges into the left lane. With the rain and the afternoon traffic another two hours away, he figures he'll be across the bridge in thirty minutes, have her in the Oakland hills in another fifteen. All told, he should be at the Hilton on Embarcadero right on schedule. He might even have time to swing by the Thai joint off the 101 freeway for spring rolls.

They are more or less silent as they leave the city. The woman adjusts herself in her seat and shakes out her damp hair. The leather seat groans and squeaks under her. She asks him to turn off the sports radio, and he turns it down. She digs in her bag, the contents rustling with little clicks and clanks every time her arm dives deeper. She unbuttons her coat and wiggles out of it noisily. Sully waits for it, and sure enough, out comes the cell phone. She talks loud enough for him to hear: "Oh, Chella, Chicago was terrible. I couldn't come to any kind of agreement with him...There's simply no talking to him about any of it... Of course they didn't want me to fly...You wouldn't believe the paperwork just to board! On top of that, the production was atrocious...You wouldn't believe. The theater was so cramped my ankles swelled up in an hour...I'd rather deliver vaginally than sit through another Molière venture..."

From the mirror Sully sees that she's huge, big-as-a-house pregnant, as Suze would say. Lately Suze has been pointing out the pregnant ladies at the grocery store. She buys the gossip rags and reads about Hollywood actresses popping the munchkins out. It has been on her mind lately, Sully can tell, that they never had kids. Sully's buddy Chuck says it's "the change"—says his wife got a little funny once she hit fifty. Sully knows it's not that, it's Cherise. Suze's sisters had no problems in the baby department, and so it was assumed that Sully's soldiers weren't up to the task. Suze never says anything about it, doesn't blame him, at least not out loud. Just last week, Sully came home and saw Suze watching their niece asleep, curled up on the love seat with the TV still on. Suze took in breaths real slow, with her hand pressed tightly to the hallway frame, and she walked away from Sully when he came up behind her.

Off the bridge and onto land, the five-lane traffic slows and stops and slowly starts again. Inching into Oakland, Sully ignores the woman as best he can and thinks about dinner tonight—Suze always bakes chicken on Tuesdays—and how tomorrow night Cherise will bring that boyfriend over for dinner. He will eat three helpings of everything and scrape the platters clean, and he and Cherise will go on and on in Arabic while Suze grins and Sully chews. Sully's seen worse, been worse himself, but still, he feels like he's on watch. Since Cherise moved up from Reno, Sully has started thinking about her like a daughter, even though most times it feels like he's wearing a borrowed hat that's too snug around the brim. Cherise moved in at the beginning of fall when she was accepted at Cal Berkeley. She took up linguistics because of that boyfriend, something Sully's been meaning to have a talk with her about, how she shouldn't get too wrapped up in some guy.

She's a good kid, though: she found an office job at her campus, and she's always studying her textbooks. Cherise wants to be a translator, and she's forever rattling off some phrase or string of words, every English word followed with one in Arabic. Sometimes it sounds like a penny sliding and clinking around in a glass jar, the way she speaks: *Good morning, Aunt, good evening, Uncle. Coffee, apple, car, record player.* And whenever he comes in from a smoke on the porch, *ashtray.* Suze laughs and laughs at this.

If Suze were here, she'd be ticking off questions about the pregnancy to the woman sitting rigidly and speaking coldly into her phone. She'd ask when she was due, was it a boy or girl, what the name would be. Her eyes would get real big and real small at the same time; her eyes become little slits when she can't stop smiling. She'd want to know all the things about the birth that were as far removed from Sully's life as Cherise's Arabic.

They are edging toward downtown on the overpass; the rain has slowed the movements of the whole freeway, with brake lights forming in bunches like a clot lodging and then dislodging down a narrow artery.

"Oh…Oh, Jesus."

Sully hears the woman, though her voice barely registers over the engine and the rain. He waits a beat, glances in the rearview. He sees only her hair.

"Everything okay back there?" Sully says.

"You have to get around this traffic." The woman readjusts in her seat. She slides to the other side of the cab, then moves back to her original position.

"What's wrong?"

"You have to drive faster," she commands in a hoarse voice. Sully turns back to see the woman's head hanging, her folds of brown hair bobbing slightly with the slow creep of the car.

"What, are you having it right now?" Sully says. And then he realizes that she is, she must be, what else could it be? A heat rises in Sully's chest, and his body pushes against the seat belt as if the townie were being slammed into from the left side. All lanes are crawling. The red lights stare back at him. He leans on the horn for lack of anything else to do. A chorus of horns responds from behind and in front and across five lanes.

"Turn around! Take me to UCSF!"

Sully motions to the wall of rain and red lights. He tries to think of a polite way of saying "Imfuckingpossible."

"I can't maneuver to the other side of the bridge."

She seems to have bigger things on her mind, because she doesn't respond for a while, what seems like hours. Traffic opens up intermittently, and Sully slams on and off the brake with each opportunity to move. He can hear the woman jostling in the backseat, and finally she shouts, "Lay off the lead-foot shit!"

He closes his eyes for a second, and he remembers his father's advice about the eggshell under the brake, how to gently push on the foot pedals or else an imaginary eggshell would crack. He wonders if she's in pain or just in shock. In the back he can hear her panting in that short-short-long, short-short-long pattern he'd seen on TV. It all seems to be happening too quickly; he had assumed that birth was a slow process with time between stages to adjust, to prepare. He doesn't know anything about it personally, and he's acutely aware of it for the first time in his life.

"Hey, don't do that in here!" The words leave his mouth as he realizes that some things refuse to abide by plans or orders.

The woman looks at him in the mirror, her eyes wild and pale.

Sully's hands are slick on the steering wheel. "All right... here's what's gonna happen. Highland's the closest hospital. I'm taking you there."

The woman squeaks, a hiccup of protest. "Don't you dare take me to Highland! I'm not giving birth next to some junkie in the waiting room!" she bellows, her hand gripping the backseat, straining to pull the rest of herself closer to Sully's ear. The white hospital towers are almost in sight, just a few blocks from the highway. Sully accelerates toward the Park Boulevard off-ramp. He turns to the backseat for a second. The woman's face is red and flushed, and the windows around her have fogged into a strange halo around her head. Her hands are gnarled knots pressed together, as if she could keep the baby inside long enough to get out of the townie and anywhere but East Oakland. Sully's eyes dart between the red lights in front of him and the blue eyes behind him.

"Not up for discussion," he sputters. Traffic opens up in the right lane, and Sully dives in and speeds until he's following the Cadillac in front of them by no more than a foot or so.

The woman rolls her head back against the headrest and mumbles. "I had three weeks. I had three more weeks..." She is either half laughing or half crying, Sully can't tell which. Her belly seems to be pushing farther and farther out, and Sully is sure if he turns to look he'll get damp pink cashmere and a protruding navel in his eye.

Christ, Sully thinks. *I should have picked up the suit in the next terminal.*

Her phone chirps. She shakes out her hair and answers, her voice strong and almost steady. "Elliot...Elliott. Shut up. It's starting...Yes, I know...Some cab...Stop your babbling and page Dr. Hennepin. You're a sack of shit, Elliot! No, he's taking me to Highland. Against my wishes." Her voice growls on the last phrase.

Sully gases it down the off-ramp and nails the brake hard at an intersection—the egg would have cracked.

"Stop praying and get it together, Elliot! Do what you have to do! Have the team on standby, and get someone over to Highland to get me!" She slaps the phone shut and reels in the backseat, her breaths heavy and loud.

Damn it, Sully thinks, his wheels squealing with the rain as he sails through a red light. *Damn it, damn it, damn it.* It becomes a mantra in his head as soon as the smell hits him. It's damp and hovers in his nostrils, and it smells like sex and sweat and mucus and something else that he can't quite name, a smell that he isn't supposed to know anything about. The scent is faint, but it sits heavy in the air. It reminds him of when he was younger and he could go with Suze all night, the sheets under their bodies damp. He thinks about the leather seats and the thick carpeting on the floor of the back. "God damn it." He finally says it aloud.

"Fuck you!" the woman howls.

Sully accelerates. "Just keep your knees together and fucking don't push!" he says more loudly than he means to. He turns a hard right onto East Thirty-first and up the short hill to the ambulance bay. His hands are wrapped tight around the steering wheel, as tightly as he imagines the woman is holding on to her belly.

He maneuvers around the open doors of an ambulance and stops under the concrete enclosure near the entrance. The rain running off the beige stucco canopy makes Sully feel like he's under the ledge of a waterfall. He throws the car in park and scrambles out of the townie, runs into the waiting room, and is almost too out of breath to shout, "Some lady is having a baby in my car!" He commandeers a wheelchair out of an orderly's gloved hands. When he gets back outside with the orderly in tow, the woman has already kicked the passenger door open and is trying to roll herself out. One of her heels has come off and is rocking on its side on the floor of the car. The seat leather is shiny wet, not in puddles but a trail.

The orderly and two security guards ease the woman onto a quickly produced gurney, and she begins barking at them as they wheel her through the emergency room entrance. "Get my bags from that son-of-a-bitch cab driver!" is the last thing he hears before the glass doors slide shut. The orderly is still outside, and Sully opens the trunk and slumps her luggage into the wheelchair. He surveys the damage as the orderly rolls her bags into the hospital. Looking at the soggy interior and the tan heel that remain, Sully realizes he wasn't paid. If there were ever a time he'd earned his fare, this was it. He sniffs the back and detects that body smell, mixing with the humidity.

"Hey, you got any towels or anything?" Sully turns to the orderly, but he is already inside and the doors have already closed.

AUTO BOB'S ON Seminary doesn't have the dazzling array of leather cleaners Sully assumed they'd carry, and the only leather shop he can think of offhand, one on International Boulevard, is closed. At the 7-Eleven, he buys a pack of Parliaments and lets the engine idle in the lot, watching the rain clouds crack and drift across the puddles in the parking lot. He decides to call Chuck, who runs a dry cleaner shop on High Street. As he drives, his fists work the steering wheel until there are hot patches under his palms. He went through a package of paper towels wiping up the backseat before the ambulance drivers told him to move the townie out. He asked one of the EMTs what they did if a woman's water breaks in the ambulance, and the EMT just laughed and said she requisitions a new gurney.

That smell won't let up, even with all four windows rolled down. It's clinging to the upholstery, and the seat still feels sticky when he reaches back to touch it. There's a smudge on the seat where the woman sat, and Sully's not sure if there's really a slight discoloration on the material or if he's being paranoid. The damp patch of mottled black looks vaguely reddish, like a splotch of bleach that was allowed to sit on the leather too long. He checks his watch—he has seventy-five minutes to take care of the smell and the wet and be at the Hilton to take Mr. Ferdinand back to his condo in the Sunset. The only bright side is that the rain has let up.

As he parks in front, Sully can see Chuck arguing with his new cashier. Chuck drops the laundry tickets on the counter when he sees Sully through the window, his one gold tooth shining. It's been a few weeks—they haven't seen each other since they went to Cache Creek last payday. Sully relays the tale, then points to the backseat. Chuck goes out to look in the back, rubs the stubble on his chin, and laughs hard before bringing out a handful of terry cloth towels and a solution in a spray bottle for Sully to try.

Sully goes at the floor first, giving the carpet a generous series of sprays and a thorough scrub. After ten minutes, three scrubs, and several of Chuck's towels, Sully sticks his nose an inch from the carpet, inhaling deep until he's almost dizzy. His back aches from hunching, and he decides to step out and stand up straight while considering how to go about cleaning the actual seat. He consults Chuck on the broader points of leather care. Chuck tells him to spray and wipe, all the while tossing the woman's high heel from hand to hand.

"Trolling the tarmac again?" Chuck sucks his teeth and taps a Kool out of the pack, points a filter toward Sully. "So where are you two heading? San Pab? Chumash?"

Sully leans against the trunk, takes the cigarette, and lights up. "Supposed to go to Reno this weekend. Suze and I are gonna drive up Friday afternoon. Cherise too." Sully makes a point of exhaling fully before turning back into the cab for another survey of the scene. It's almost time to go and fetch Mr. Ferdinand. He's not sure what will piss the old man off more, the smell of smoke or the smell of birth. The suit will probably make him take the car back, probably bitch to Mendoza, the new supervisor, and the face of the new management firm. Mendoza has already been on Sully about the mileage on the odometer and the gas receipts he's turned in. Sully suddenly wishes he'd made a point of getting paid. It was the least the preggers could have done.

"You making a weekend of it?" Chuck asks and looks toward the clouds breaking in light and dark patches. He coughs a puff of smoke. He and Sully smoked their first cigarettes together at Oakland High.

"Well, we've been meaning to go up for a while, and Cherise wants to visit her folks. There's that new poker section at the Horseshoe, so that'll be good. And you know Suze is all over the machines. Regular family vacation," Sully says, and catches himself in the kind of chuckle that only comes when you say something that surprises yourself. He turns and sprays the solution again into the back. It smells vaguely like soap and overripe fruit.

Sully swirls the towel across the leather in figure eights. Suze loves Reno; Sully tries to take her every few months. Her sister, Cherise's mother, lives up there, and they always visit, but really Suze loves the slots, can stay plugged into one for hours. "You remember that trip last spring? She played a quarter that got her six hundred dollars. She was jumping around like a kid, and I'll be damned if most of it didn't go straight back into that same machine." Sully works at the spot on the leather, watching the seat give slightly with every swipe of the towel. "She found a machine she thought liked her, and she stuck with it until her six hundred got whittled down to two. She didn't want to be far from the lucky machine that had paid out, so the rest went into the next slot over. We didn't make a dime that trip."

Sully inches out of the back and finds his cigarette balanced on the edge of the shop's window. He inhales and thinks that same logic is probably what keeps Suze with him—Sully was a good bet once, and she's too loyal or too stubborn to admit that he didn't pay out the way he was supposed to. No kids, a pissant pension, and they are still living in the same house on Twenty-sixth Street, the house that they were supposed to move out of once he got a management job at the shipping yard and they had their first batch of rug rats. But Sully was let go from the warehouse during the last round of cuts, and he and Suze were too busy staying afloat themselves to think about adding a small squealing mouth to feed. He'd taken the job driving the townie as a quick fix, just like she took on extra hours at the dress shop, but the rough patch became the long stretch. The years slipped by like pulls on the handle, one after another until you looked at your empty quarter bucket and wondered if you really were at that same machine the whole time.

The cigarette is nothing but filter, and Sully tosses it into the gutter.

Chuck cranes his neck into the cab. "When you think luck's on your side, you get superstitious," he says. *He would know,* Sully thinks—Chuck wears the same pair of black ribbed socks every time they go to Reno, or even just to the casino in San Pablo. Sully nods. He keeps his father's billfold in his back left pocket whenever he plays craps. Suze always wears her silver shoes, those flats he bought for her so many trips ago from an outlet store on the way back from Vegas. The heels are worn down and there are creases bent deep into the patent leather, but she still wears them every single time.

Sully takes off his black cap, scratches his head, and then pulls it back on snug. "You smell anything?"

"I think you're pretty fucked, my friend," Chuck laughs. When Sully doesn't join him, he straightens out, inhales loud and deep enough for Sully to hear, and then shakes his head. Nonetheless, he goes into his shop and comes out with another spray bottle.

"Fabric refresher. Maybe it'll work the same as it does on mothball smell."

WHEN CHERISE FIRST moved in and Sully was still figuring out how to have an eighteen-year-old in the house after twenty-six years of just him and Suze, the easiest thing to talk about was school. They'd sit across from each other in the kitchen or the living room, him in his easy chair and her on the couch— regardless of where she was, her books were always spread out around her. He'd ask what she was studying, and she'd prattle on in Arabic a while, occasionally finding a clean piece of paper and writing in thick lines and abrupt curls. Sully would smile, nod, then ask about what else she was learning. She talked about her psychology class and how every morning her professor told the class to be quiet for a few minutes and visualize how they wanted things to happen that day. Sully had thought it sounded like horseshit, but Cherise looked so earnest, her eyes closed and her lips bent in a half smile as she talked about imagining Arabic words flying from her mouth in her voice. She said every morning she visualized the calligraphy flowing out of her pen as if it were a geyser spewing ink.

"Masha'allah," she had said and smoothed the curled edges of her notebook, and Sully felt like he should have understood her, that he'd heard her say the word so many times he should have picked it up by osmosis. But she saved him, didn't make him ask her again what it meant. "What God wills, Uncle Sully, what

God wants," she had said, then turned back to her notebook and scribbled out the word for him to see.

"Masha'allah," he breathes as he rounds the corner onto Embarcadero, all the windows down, his neck cold. He says it like he remembers Cherise saying it, thick on the first syllable, his voice as sure as hers would be. He hopes he is saying it right.

He is thirteen minutes early to pick up Mr. Ferdinand. When he pulls up to the curb and throws the townie into park, he reluctantly takes another look in the backseat. The leather has been buffed and sprayed and buffed again, and he wonders if the woman's baby has already been born or if it is still laboring into the world, its lungs still content in water.

As the second hand ticks loudly from his watch he tries to visualize: the wetness will have dried completely, and there will be no trace of the smell, carried away by Chuck's miracle spray and the push of the bay winds. Mr. Ferdinand emerges from the revolving glass doors, his steps deliberate and his copy of the *Times* folded neatly under his arm. He will enter the back without comment, and perhaps halfway to the Sunset he will ask Sully who he's been banging on company time, and then he'll laugh and turn back to the paper. Sully will drop off the townie at the garage on Harrison, Mendoza will have gone home for the day, and there will be no traffic on the way back to Twenty-sixth Street.

Suze and Cherise will just be serving the chicken legs, greens, and potatoes when Sully walks in the door. He will come home and they will eat and he will ask the girls if they are excited to go to Reno. What time should they leave on Friday, or should they drive up early Saturday? Sully won't mind doing the lion's share of the driving, and the highway through the mountains will be salted and clear of snow. When they get there, he'll have cash for them—tens and twenties to press into their palms like secrets—and he'll tell them to have fun, go shopping. Cherise will thank him in Arabic, and he will understand her, say "Masha'allah," and Cherise will guffaw and be impressed. Suze will pinch his left earlobe, kiss his right cheek, and click her silver heels together for luck, as she always does before she heads to the slots.

THE FRONT OF
THE HOUSE

ELSIE CAREENED OFF Seminary into the parking lot, maneuvering across the potholes to the spot farthest from the restaurant entrance. The parking lot was inordinately full at this hour. A bad omen: too many people far too early. Stretching her arms until her palms grazed the ceiling, Elsie watched a couple move across the parking lot in her rearview mirror. They were Indian, the man in a dark blue suit, and the woman in a canary-yellow sari, her braid swaying with the folds of her scarf. The man held his hand against the small of her back, and the woman leaned toward his ear to whisper something, and Elsie felt her eyes narrow as she turned away.

It's been six days since she spoke to Manuel, since she finally found the nerve to say, "Don't go to Vegas. Don't marry that girl. Be with me. You love me, don't you?" She didn't say that last part, just thought it, and he didn't answer her, just looked out at the marina. They sat on a park bench, the afternoon sun wavering behind the fog and the bay smooth and flat as a steel sheet. Her legs were propped across his lap, and he rested one hand on her thigh and ran the other from her ankle to her knee, back and forth.

A brisk knock on the passenger window startled her, and there was Lorena, looking at Elsie through the dirty window.

Elsie unlocked the door, but Lorena didn't slip into the passenger seat.

"We need you inside right now," Lorena said, bending her neck into the body of the Impala.

"Am I late?"

Lorena shook her head and worked her hands up and down across her black pinstriped thighs. "Someone fucked up with the time. The guests are here."

Elsie checked her watch—a futile gesture. "Now? Are we set up?"

Lorena dropped her chin against her chest in exasperation. "Chinta and I just got the tables up. The host is here. They already want drinks."

If Elsie had half an hour to arrange her station, it would have been fine. The last thing she needed was to serve while setting. Each task would take twice as long and be twice as aggravating. "Where's Ramesh? I could kill that fool."

"He's at a party in Sacramento. He left Jack in charge tonight for some reason. All the waitresses are at that party in Sacto, or they can't make it."

Elsie grabbed her bag and reached in the back to shake her pressed white button-up off its hanger. "Is Leti around? Or Cece? Maybe one of them can come through."

Lorena was already halfway across the parking lot. "It's just us tonight."

At the back door, Lorena waited while Elsie slid her white shirt over her wifebeater, the starched sleeves covering the brocade of tattoos on both arms.

The hot air of the kitchen rose up to meet them, the smells of oil and coal and raw chicken and garlic heavy in their noses.

Elsie shouted hello over the roar of the tandoor ovens—the cooks smiled or waved and turned just as quickly back to their tasks—and made her way across the dining room floor to the bar. About fifty guests milled around the restaurant. Chinta, the other waitress, threw tablecloths over the round tables, and Lorena ran over and began placing floral centerpieces at each covered table. Men in tailored suits and colored silk shirts were already ringing the bar, and Elsie tried to hide her grimace with a forced, toothy grin.

It was a simple bar: olive linoleum countertop with some cupboards below, a metal sink against the wall. Three cardboard boxes sat on the bar top, filled haphazardly with two-liter bottles of whiskey and gin and plastic bottles of club soda. A row of elbows and forearms planted themselves on the bar top, and a voice behind them chuckled, "All right, she's here!"

Elsie retightened her smile. "Give me ten minutes, gents," she said as she pulled the first box off the counter. The younger men sighed and grunted. Already they were impatient, and already Elsie was irritated. "I'll grab some ice and fix you all up."

She exited the bar and made her way toward the kitchen, but instead of heading to the ice machine, she ducked into the bathroom, shut the door, and leaned against it, glad that the sounds of the restaurant and the guests were muffled like a television show blaring in the next room. Her bag was still slung over her shoulder. She hadn't had a moment to toss it under her station. The guests would have to wait regardless, so she rolled her neck, fluffed her hair in the mirror, and dug through her purse to find the lipsticks. That afternoon she had been shopping to occupy her time and her mind, and she found herself in the makeup aisle. She never wore lipstick when she was with Manuel. One day he told her that he liked her lips and nothing else, that when he kissed her, he wanted to taste only her. After that, she hadn't touched any of her makeup.

The lipstick was an impulse, a physical reaction: Manuel had not called, he was marrying that girl, her lips were terribly dry. She tore open each package and unfurled each tube— Candy Apple, Sultry Autumn, Burgundy Splash. Considering each color, she drew in slow, deliberate breaths, and dotted each of the lipstick tips against the back of her hand. She decided on Burgundy Splash, dark and rich. She rolled the tube across her lips, pressed, puckered, then blotted against the Chinese character for luck tattooed on the inside of her right wrist.

JACK STOOD IN front of the water-stained bathroom mirror under the flickering bulb, listening to the murmur of voices and the shuffle of footsteps in the dining room. He tightened the bulb in its hanging socket, and then looked himself over in the now-steady light. He pinched a lonely black hair between his eyebrows and pulled, then examined his teeth and checked his breath. Overlooking the shadows under his eyes, he felt presentable: he had shaved and slicked his hair back, and he put on the gold chain gifted to him from his wife when he left Delhi for San Francisco. The chain sometimes caught on a hair on his chest and pulled, but he wore it even though it might pinch throughout the evening.

Rolling up his sleeves to hide the yellow curry spots on his shirt cuffs, he looked the part tonight, more like a manager than a waiter. Professional. Ramesh had left him in charge, and it was his first night running an event entirely by himself. He smoothed a wrinkle in his collar with a bit of cold water on his fingertips, wiped down the wet countertop with a paper towel, and stepped out onto the restaurant floor.

The waitresses ran from table to table, their arms full of wadded tablecloths. The DJ plugged in the speakers, and feedback erupted intermittently. The old ladies covered their ears, either scowling or laughing with each static burst. Elsie the bartender was unloading whiskey bottles, chatting up the men waiting for drinks. It was barely six o'clock and already the cooks were shouting at one another, and there wasn't the loud throbbing of bhangra to cover up the arguing and clang of pots on the concrete kitchen floor. Jack strode across the room, avoiding the cluster of arrivals. They could all be greeted later.

The head cook, Assam, held a large dented wok in his hands, while Ripu held another wok that was smaller but still had its proper shape. They shouted back and forth in Urdu, something about the spinach. Jack could get along fine when the cooks were joking; he could piece together what they were saying through his own Hindi dialect. But in anger, Urdu was like the Pakistani mountains, rough and jagged in his ears, making a rock of his tongue. Jack raised his hands against the loud grunts and woks hovering in the air, ready to be thrown. "Settle down, settle down! What's the problem?"

"Ramesh told us seven! We planned to be prepped by seven!" Assam shouted, his fat arm cutting through a swath of rising steam. All of the burners on all three stoves glowed with orange-blue life. "This is shit!" Assam said in English. He only used English for cursing.

A braid of sweat formed at Jack's hairline, and he checked the clock and the movements of the guests through the doorway.

The sun hadn't set yet. They could serve the cold dishes first, and then another wave of hot dishes, as if all part of the plan. The waitresses were still hurrying through the room, dodging the toddlers running around the last set of bare tables. The guests were already at the set tables, rearranging chairs and unfurling the cloth napkins that had been folded in the water glasses, waiting for someone to fill their glass. He smoothed the front of his shirt. He could salvage this. It would be as if this hour was never lost in the first place.

He assigned Ripu the task of making pistachio candies, and put Emilio and Santo to work chopping wedges of melon and cucumbers and limes on a silver platter. Assam grumbled as he fried up the fish pakora, and Ripu hunched over a slab of burfi, cutting the hardened paste into diamonds. Jack found an extra batch of chilled lentils from yesterday's buffet and poured the soup into a tureen. In fifteen minutes, they had four dishes to send out to the guests and a window of time to finish the hot hors d'oeuvres. The kitchen was as quiet as it ever was with the cooks in their corners and the gas burners humming behind a chorus of chopping knives and sizzling meat.

Stepping onto the main floor, Jack supposed it didn't really matter who had gotten the time wrong: Ramesh or the host or the cooks or the guests. Whatever the circumstances, he was ready. He could change plans and improvise, make everything work. Even if one of the stoves broke or they didn't have enough meat for the curries or the cooks were too angry or drunk to prepare the food on time or in the right proportions, Jack could run things without the host ever knowing of the chaos in the kitchen.

This was one of the more aggravating aspects of his work at DiRaji's, that his title as "Waiter" in no way reflected the nature of his responsibilities. A waiter takes orders, serves food, and brings out the check. He would like to have a title like those he'd seen in the want ads: "Service Manager" was more appropriate, or perhaps "Event Organizer" or "Food Director." These sounded good to him. Important.

The guests were spreading out, claiming tables, clustering into groups. Children in miniature suits and puffy skirts raced across the empty dance floor. About half of the expected two hundred people had arrived, and the rest would be there soon, no doubt. The host was Gurinder Varma, the owner of several commercial buildings and most recently a car dealership in Union City. Many Punjabs and Sikhs from all over the Bay Area had come to talk business and visit and bask in the display of Gurinder Varma's success. They always came in droves for a birthday or feast day or, like today, a wedding—one of Varma's relations and a bride who had just arrived from Punjab. Usually Jack didn't like these country parties, where so many people were old-timers. Sometimes he caught an arched brow or a narrow eye when he spoke to the guests, as if they could tell by his accent or his face or his stance that he was really from Delhi, that his first tongue was Hindi. They looked at him and seemed to rear back, as if they could smell the stink of the river on him, across the world or the room.

Varma ambled toward the buffet as Jack ladled mint sauce and tamarind chutney into tureens. He wore a gray linen suit with a garish maroon tie, anchored to his shirt by a golden lion's head pin. His black hair puffed at the back of his neck, and his cheeks were high and rosy over a thin smile. Elsie the bartender would say Varma had a shit-eating grin. Jack smiled at the thought.

"Where are the samosas? I ordered samosas and pakora for the appetizers." Varma adjusted his cuff link and grabbed a pistachio candy off the tray. He spoke again with his mouth full. "And why aren't the wedding chairs ready? The couple should be arriving shortly." Varma pointed at the partition in the center of the dining room: a swath of gold and white fabric was wrapped around two poles, forming a canopy over two yellow armchairs with elaborate wood carvings on the backs and legs. Varma's wife and daughter floated around the platform, waiting for the waitresses to finish arranging the display before adding bunches of flowers.

"The chairs will be ready in five minutes. And we've prepared two rounds of appetizers, first cold dishes, and then hot," Jack said without skipping a beat. "It's so warm today, we find that the cold entrees are best until sunset. Then the hot entrees and then dinner at nine...or so." Jack said this last part as Varma turned to greet an old man with a scraggly white beard.

"If you require anything, I'm in charge," Jack said to Varma's back. The two men strode away from the buffet table. Varma wasn't complaining, which was a good thing, Jack decided. In the front of the house, everything appeared seamless. The disorder and confusion was out of sight in the back rooms, behind curtains and swinging doors.

Someone pushed on his shoulders from behind. Jack turned to Elsie.

"Jack! Come help me at the bar. Get them off my back for a minute." Elsie grabbed his elbow and pulled him toward the bar, pointing at the congregation of men waiting to be served. Jack went to arrange the liquor bottles and sodas while Elsie lined up several cups, then poured ice and an even stream of whiskey into each. As he arranged the beers in the ice bed and tucked scotch and gin bottles into the cupboards, he watched her movements become methodical, her hands quick and sure among the tipping bottles. The men barked as Elsie prepared the drinks: "Crown neat." "Crown with soda." "Three Heinekens and a black and Coke." "Black Label, no ice. I said no ice!"

Whatever they said, she smiled and responded, "Of course, coming right up, sir." She swept ice into a cup with one hand, with the bottle poised to pour in the other. "There you go, sir. Enjoy." Jack sliced lime wedges, and she grabbed them as soon as they were cut and dropped them into cups. The handoff of drinks complete, and the dollars secured in the tip jar, Elsie tucked a brown curl behind her ear and turned to the next face in the crowd.

Jack liked watching her at the bar, pivoting on her foot and finding the right bottles and mixers by habit. Of all the bartenders, she was his favorite: when he first arrived at DiRaji's two years ago, she humored him and helped with his terrible English. She taught him curse words and phrases, and explained the expressions he had heard but couldn't make sense of in American movies. When the parties were slow, they shared garlic naan and she would ask about Delhi and the Ganges River, the Gods and the Om tattoos that some of the old men who came to the parties had on the backs of their hands. All the cooks were in love with her, and some nights, he lingered behind the kitchen curtain and watched her dance to the bhangra behind the bar.

After twenty minutes, the first wave of drinkers passed, and Elsie leaned against the sink as Jack covered the beers with a fresh layer of ice.

"I hate it when they all show up at once," Elsie muttered. She took a bar napkin off the stack and dabbed it against her forehead. "Makes me feel like I'm playing catch-up the whole night."

Jack nodded and stood up straight. "We'll get through easy," he said, and stepped out from the bar. "No sweat."

Elsie shook her head and called after him, "Easy for you, Jack! I'm not used to slaving!" He turned to her and whirled a finger at his temple—a motion she had taught him.

A blare of feedback roared and then subsided as bhangra burst through the hall. Lorena and Chinta walked about the dining room, placing sweating jugs of ice water at each table. A line of guests waited to pick at the cold appetizers, and Varma was still working the crowd. He hadn't come over to badger Jack about the food or the music or the air-conditioning or any of the other things that a host might find to complain about. Jack looked around the restaurant, at the battered tables covered with white sheets to hide their age, the scuff marks worn into the tile. Just beneath the edge of the wallpaper border of gold fleur-de-lis, the white paint was cracking. *Tomorrow,* Jack thought, *I'll mix some glue with warm water and paste the border back down, so no one will see the cracks in the paint and the little slices of plaster peeking through.* Sometimes Jack would find a chip of paint that had drifted from the wall and landed on him when he was serving, and he would quickly pick it off his shirt or out of his hair before serving the next plate.

AN HOUR INTO the party, Elsie knew this was going to be one of *those* nights, where the cash felt greasy and her back would ache the next day. In her illustrious four-year stint as freelance bartender, Elsie had her fair share of bullshit gigs where the cash at the end of the night in no way made up for the hassle of the gig itself: rowdy customers, unexpected shortages of vital bar supplies (say the only bottle opener breaks or the host brings ten bottles of liquor and two bottles of mixer, or one sad bag of ice), or the classic anal-retentive host, who is positive that someone is going to steal liquor and so insists on cataloguing the empties and measuring the open bottles. Not to mention the dogs, the men who staked out a barstool and hounded Elsie for her number throughout the evening until she finally scribbled a fake one on a bar napkin so they would stop leering and leave. Nights like these, each dollar in the jar had a film of sweat and dirt that wanted to seep into her fingers at the end of the shift.

Tonight was the worst kind of open bar—a mixed party of businessmen from all over the Bay Area, the crowd heavy with bachelors and only peppered with married couples. Some were making sure to drink heavy since the booze was free. Elsie made drinks and did her best to crack jokes and laugh in kind at theirs, only half hearing the men between the loud bhangra and their thick accents. One of her favorite things about the parties when she began working for DiRaji's three years back was listening to the men speaking Punjabi as she poured drinks. When they spoke, the quick chopping sound of the speech made Elsie imagine overflowing creeks, the sound of water alternating between crisp splashes and low murmurs of constant movement. Jack had taught her the essentials—*Yes. No. Where? Hurry up! Too hot. How many?*—but she could never remember the curse words and expressions Jack had taught her that might come in handy with guests who got too drunk, too fast.

As she poured drinks and laughed with the men gathered around, Elsie saw a few of the wives at the tables, their faces sour and their arms crossed over their chests. Huddled together, they stared down the bar: a squat woman in a hot pink sari, a shriveled grandma with thick-rimmed glasses, and a young woman in a bright yellow sari with gold beading, the woman she'd seen in the parking lot. What must have been her husband stood at the corner of the bar, a lanky Punjab with slicked hair and a blue jacket made of rough silk. *Blue bird, yellow bird, funny pairing,* Elsie thought as she veered toward his end of the bar. Manuel had a bluebird holding a banner in its beak with his mother's name in script tattooed on his torso.

The Punjab ordered two Black Label shots, and he took one from her hand and said, "That one is for you." He was young, and he leaned against the counter, smiling.

Elsie went to wipe down the bar top in circles, making sure not to look at the boy. She made a point of not drinking when she bartended. The quicker she poured, the better the tips, and booze only slowed her down, made her hands less precise and her pours too heavy. "I'm not supposed to."

The boy hung his head as if he'd been shot. "Come on, beautiful. You can have whatever you want."

Elsie looked at him, considering the gelled sprig of hair pointing up from his forehead and the ghost of stubble on his chin. Ramesh wasn't around, and Jack was busy in the kitchen. Another batch of men were making their way toward the bar. Since the drink was in her hand and since his smile was somewhat like Manuel's—the left side of his lips curled to reveal long teeth—she shrugged and touched glasses with the boy. When she tilted her head upright, the wife in canary yellow stared straight at her behind the young man's shoulders. Elsie smiled, despite herself. She turned away from the boy, who had pointed to his empty cup for a refill.

A burst of drums blasted from the speaker, interrupting the

chatter in the busy room. At last, the bride and groom arrived through the front doors. The groom was young and chubby, in a cream dress coat with a maroon sash and a matching turban. The bride followed two steps behind, holding a trailing piece of fabric from the groom's turban in her hands. She looked tiny in the massive draping of her red wedding gown, sparkling with yellow sequins. A thin chain connected the gold barrette in the part of her hair to her left nostril and threaded to one of her bracelets. Saddled around her neck was a chain with huge gold balls the size of oranges that hung past her waist.

"Ladies and gentlemen, may I introduce to you…" The DJ riffled through a few pieces of paper, then dropped them and turned back to the microphone. "May I introduce the happy new couple!" All of the guests turned and politely clapped. The DJ put on a softer song with reed flutes and a soaring female voice, and the guests stood and filed toward the buffet as the cooks wheeled the dinner trays out.

The couple arranged themselves in the armchairs in the center of the room. Neither smiled as the photographer took their picture. Elsie watched as the flashbulb burst, casting a bolt of white on the wall behind them. Her sari was beautiful, the red making her brown skin stark and luminous. If Elsie were to marry, she would not wear a white gown, but a red one like the Indian brides, deep red like thick blood, with beading all along the torso and sleeves, and gold affixed to her ears, her neck, her fingers, her nose, the part in her hair. She laughed at that thought, that someone might marry her, and a wave rolled through her as if Manuel were behind her, his arms finding their way around her waist.

A pair of headlamps pulling into the parking lot caught her

eye, and she instinctively scanned the parking lot for Manuel's truck. The dark evening spread itself over the hills, dotted with the shimmer of streetlamps and low beams. Of course he wasn't there, and she chastised herself for even looking. It was too early. If he were coming, he wouldn't arrive until he closed up the shop at ten in two hours. He was probably already in Vegas at some tacky chapel, marrying that girl. Instinctively she pulled down her sleeves so her tattoos couldn't peek out from her rolled-up cuffs. She wondered what a bride in Vegas might don on her big day—a stretched satin bodice and ripped jeans, stiletto pumps, a liquor-store daisy bouquet. Or maybe something too formal for a quickie chapel: a gown of tailored silk, amid cotton shirts with tuxedo prints and pink plastic sixty-six-ounce beer cups. She poured a half shot of whiskey and didn't bother to hide behind the counter as she drank it.

Manuel had loved her tattoos; he'd lay in the curve of her side, tracing over them with his fingers, as if he were drawing them again. That was how she met him, when she happened into a shop in Alameda looking to get the calla lily on her bicep retouched with undertones of yellow and white and blue. Manuel was brawny, thick-armed, with an Aztec face, and had black hair pulled in a topknot. She liked the intricate red and black rings around his forearms, the firmness with which he cupped her arm, how his left eyebrow jumped up every time he laughed. He plastered a piece of Saran wrap over her arm and asked her out for a drink, his eyes never leaving hers. She didn't try hard to find a reason to say no.

They went across the street to McGinty's, killed a bottle of white tequila between them, and after speeding erratically across town to the Berkeley marina, they smoked two blunts and kissed all night. She would have fucked him had it not been for the throbbing of her arm and the cramped back of the Impala. Instead of pawing at her pants, he kissed her mouth, her neck, her knees, the soft skin around her navel, all the places that made her shiver and writhe underneath him. She thought of that first kiss, how he drew close to her and then paused. She thought it had been so sexy, almost chivalrous, at the time. Now, with the few drops of whiskey swirling in the bottom of her cup, she wondered if just before their lips first met, he thought of his fiancée, felt her hand on his shoulder, his real life already pulling him back.

"CHAKALA, CHAKALA! ¡MUÉVETE! Let's go!" Jack shouted above the clatter of the kitchen. The food was finally ready to be served in stainless steel vats—chicken tikka, stewed lentils, goat and lamb curries, fried okra and eggplant, curried potatoes and chickpeas, basmati rice, and stacks of fresh naan. Dinner was supposed to have been served forty-five minutes ago, but the guests were still dancing and the men were still drinking, and the extra batch of samosas that Jack had sent out had appeased the heckles for dinner. As soon as the cooks poured their curries and vegetables into the pans, Jack began sending the food out.

The guests abandoned their positions and made for the buffet, grabbing plates as the steaming trays were slid into place. Only a few waited for the presentation of the couple before lining up to eat, and nearly everyone was eating by the time the pictures were taken and the blessings from the parents were made. It was a moot point, Jack figured: the bride had no family here and the groom was a distant cousin to the host, but nonetheless, it seemed impolite. His own wedding was a simple affair in his wife's parents' garden, with a feast made by Jack's mother and sisters and aunts and nieces. They ate outside under the banyan trees in their courtyard surrounded by all of his relations and his Sati beside him, glowing in her bright red sari. Sati's mother had woven white crystals among the gold beads in her bodice, and he wavered with the thought of her dress in the sunlight, the sun catching the facets of the little beads and their rainbow light ricocheting every which way.

Sometimes, at the strangest moments, he had storms of memory. He'd be prepping kebabs or mopping or flirting with the waitresses and suddenly remember the slight gap between Sati's front teeth or the three moles that formed a triangle and made her hip into a soft sloping pyramid, or how her back curved as she braided her hair. But other times when he tried to conjure her, he could barely remember the sound of her voice, or if her eyes were brown or hazel. Sati sent him letters with pictures of her and her family, of their son Gupti. When his absence was still new, Sati had written love letters, but now she reported Gupti's growth and his mother's health, the goings-on in their complex in Delhi, gossip about neighbors he didn't care about then, let alone now. He would receive them, glance at them, and put them away. If he lingered on the pictures, studied the little boy's face, the vacuous center in his chest became overwhelming, unbearable, his body suddenly an empty aluminum can. So he worked, and he worked hard. He arrived at DiRaji's at eight in the morning and usually left around midnight, later on the weekends. Every day he would keep moving and stay busy, pushing his body so that whenever he returned to his room, he would collapse into sleep, hopefully before his mind had a chance to click into memory or register the painful absence.

The bride's hand was still fixed to the tail of her new husband's turban. A new husband and a new world, both of whom he was sure she had only first met a few weeks ago. He wondered if he looked so stark in the days following his arrival to California, landing with a suitcase and the letters from one of his uncle's American associates, Ramesh Diraji, who promised him a foothold, a place to stay, and a steady job. He jumped at the chance, even though Sati was four months pregnant. Jack dismissed her protests. He believed that it would take only a year to amass enough wealth and clout to bring Sati and the baby over, two at most. When he arrived, he was optimistic, full of energy to work, to make money, to rise through the ranks of Ramesh's business, maybe even start a business of his own.

Ramesh's letters did not prepare him for the life waiting for him in San Francisco. The streets were crowded and filthy, and he saw beggars and wanderers who looked more wild-eyed and ravaged than those in Delhi. Ramesh's driver did not take him to his new home but straight to the restaurant, where Jack spent his first day in America washing dishes and emptying garbage cans. It was plain to see that Ramesh's "wealthy corporation" was an Indian restaurant chain with two locations that catered almost exclusively to Punjabi community events. The levels of advancement went from dishwasher to server to cook.

After the restaurant closed that first night, Jack walked with the other cooks to the house off High Street, seven blocks from the restaurant. Sandwiched between an auto repair shop and a square plot of dry grass surrounded by chain link was a flat-top house with dry dirt for a lawn. This was Ramesh's arranged housing, and Jack was to share a room with Assam the cook, who belched and farted constantly while awake and snored incessantly when asleep. The two Mexican cooks, Santo and Emilio, occupied the other bedroom. The rest of the house was storage space for old draperies, furniture, and cooking equipment for the business. Two weeks went by before he could write a letter to Sati. Every time he put pen to paper, his fingers would cramp and he would bite his nails to the quick. How could he tell her that he was not a manager but an underling in the kitchen? Sati would hang her head if he told her of his cot in a small room and his fingers shriveled from washing dishes all day. Or worse, she would say the obvious—this is what you left your wife and child for? He worked his scalded hand over the paper: "Everything is great here. It is exactly like they said."

The DJ played one last plaintive love ballad, and then the clattering sounds of bhangra filled the restaurant again. Jack wandered around the dining room, watching the people eat and talk, occasionally sending one of the waitresses to clear a table or clean up a spill. Surveying the evening, he felt accomplished, in control: they had made up for the start-time problem, and everyone who wasn't eating was dancing. After circling the room, Jack found his way to the bar. A few men stood in a small cluster, but they were watching the dancing and their cups were full. Jack posted an elbow on the bar-top edge and put his forehead in his palm, suddenly exhausted. Elsie stepped across to him and mimicked his position. "What you want, boss?"

"Cook's special," Jack said, trying to hold back a grin.

"Since when do you drink?" Jack never drank on the job whenever she bartended. She had assumed he was one of the Hindus who didn't drink, like the guests that only asked for sodas at the bar and laughed politely with the drinkers diving headlong into their plastic cups.

Jack shook his head and looked at the dance floor. "Just a little bit. Easy party tonight," he said, and then let his smile off the reins. Sometimes he drank beers with Emilio and Santo after work, when he couldn't sleep despite his exhaustion. But tonight, he felt like he deserved a reward. Varma was moored at his table, surrounded by sloshed compatriots. The food was served. The music was crisp. The floor was crowded with people dancing under a warbling light machine. Yellow and blue and orange and pink scattered in repetitive leaps across the white walls.

"I'm glad someone's having an easy night," Elsie said as she dug a cup into the sink of watery ice. "How much longer until they clear out?"

"Probably at one o'clock we can go," Jack said, watching Elsie behind the countertop tip the bottle into his cup.

"The sooner, the better," she muttered, and discreetly passed him the drink. He took a gulp from the cup and placed it on the shelf behind the bar, the liquor burning his throat after the sweet cola faded. On the dance floor, the men were soused and dancing, jerking their arms and torsos with the music. A group of women danced in a circle, and when a man jumped into the center and fell to his knees, crooning along with the chorus, they all laughed and turned in circles, adjusting their veils on their shoulders.

"Don't they look crazy to you?" Jack asked, watching the sweaty men prance around the wooden floor, smiles plastered to their faces. Elsie shook her head.

"I like it. Fucking white folks don't ever get down like this," Elsie said, and took another sip of her drink. As she swallowed, she thought that she should leave the drink alone for a while. She could feel her reaction time widening, her movements sluggish under the pull of the alcohol. Cussing unconsciously was her personal Breathalyzer. Elsie poured a cup of ice water and drank it down in greedy gulps.

The two stood watch at the bar, resting on their elbows. Jack translated the song lyrics for Elsie, craning to catch her ear—*across rivers and mountains, do you hear my heart calling you?* Only then, as he leaned into her ear, her hair almost brushing his face, did he notice the empty wedding chairs. The new husband sat at the Varmas' table in the back. The bride was nowhere to be seen until he scanned the periphery of the dining room, her glittering sari a buoy in a sea of black and blue suits. She moved slowly and unmistakably toward the bar. There was nothing else to approach on this side of the restaurant. A cold grip of dread clenched in Jack's throat, and he cleared his throat to spirit the feeling away.

Elsie followed the path of his eyes to the bride. "What is she doing?" Women rarely ever came to the bar, only the women who were American born. And even then, they asked for wine in white Styrofoam cups, then quickly returned to their tables of other girls or onto the arm of their husband.

Jack looked to the Varmas, who hadn't taken notice of what was happening across the floor. "Don't give her anything," he hissed at Elsie.

Her head cocked back, and her smile dropped. "Why not?" She was poised to say more when the bride floated up to the counter.

She was short and seemed to slouch, working the edge of her sari in one hand. Her dark eyes darted from her own image in the foggy mirror to the bottles lined along the bar, and then to Jack, who pulled himself upright and rounded the corner to stand alongside her. Elsie moved with him, then pushed her sleeves up and looked at the bride. It struck her how tiny the woman looked in her envelope of red fabric, her face a stone, her hands a bundle of twigs.

She cleared her throat. "I want a drink," the bride said in Punjabi.

"Go ask your husband," Jack said, his tone quiet but hard. He wanted to save her the embarrassment, spare everyone a spectacle. Go back to your chair, he willed her, but it was too late: some of the guests had already turned and seen.

Elsie didn't know what was said, but she was fairly sure it wasn't good. She shook her hair a bit and leaned toward the bride. "What can I get for you?"

The bride turned to Elsie. "Drink," she said, her English sharp.

Jack's shoulders stiffened, and he looked at Elsie, his eyes shouting *Don't*. Elsie ignored him and pushed closer to the bride across the counter. Elsie softened her face and pointed at the bottles lined up. "What would you like?"

The bride nodded as her fingers grazed over the bottle of Green Label scotch. Jack growled her name, but Elsie met his gaze, her hand wrapped tight around the bottleneck.

"Everyone gets a drink at my bar." Elsie spat the words and tossed the bottle cap into the sink. Jack was livid. She could tell by the bend in his brow. But she was already pouring, and she couldn't back down, let the bride see the cup within reach, then have someone empty it, toss it away, deny that it was ever meant for her at all. The liquid splashed, and Elsie watched the bride, whose eyes had never left the drink, her hands in balled fists on the countertop.

As she placed the scotch in front of the bride, she saw in the crowd a few necks craned, lips bobbing toward others' ears. In the back, there was a rustle at the host's table, the scratch of chair legs pushed across tile. A rush of gooseflesh swept over her, anxiety bristling on her skin. Elsie gripped the bottleneck as the new husband worked his way across the floor, the host a few steps behind. The murmur of laughter and voices was alive, but falling away, making the music suddenly full and loud. Elsie wanted to say, "Drink it all now. They're coming," but she could only push out a strained whisper: "Hurry." Suddenly her body was heavy as wet wool. Both of their bodies stiffened with the thud of the men's approaching footsteps.

The bride took the cup gingerly in both hands and took a sip—one quick pass of the cup to her lips—then sighed and placed it back on the counter. Her eyes did not leave Elsie's until two sets of bulky arms slithered over her shoulders. She disappeared behind the backs of the host and her new husband.

"You ruined it, you've—" Jack said to her, then turned away and stalked across the main floor after them, his shoulders tight around his neck. Elsie bit her lower lip and looked at the near-full drink in front of her, a smudge of the bride's lipstick on the edge of the plastic cup.

No more drinks were served. Any men who were still drinking had stepped away from the bar. Elsie worked a paper napkin in her hand until it began to shred. The host and the new couple were nowhere in sight. She ducked behind the bar out of view of the patrons and finished her whiskey in a gulp, trying to soothe the tremors in her chest. She wiped the bar down in long swirls, trying to figure out if she had made the right call or if she should have turned her away, like Jack had told her to. When she drank she got too hotheaded, too impetuous, didn't think about consequences. Maybe if she were closer to sober, she could have overlooked her balled hands, her eyes both flat and roiling like a swarm of wasps.

The music didn't stop, but after a while, the guests pulled on their coats and gathered sleeping children off the chairs. Families began moving toward the double-door exits, thanking the Varmas for a wonderful evening as quickly as possible before leaving. When all of the guests were gone, the host and his family exited the restaurant silently, the bride in between two women, the groom skulking behind them. Jack began to follow the family out, but he stopped when the entrance doors slammed shut behind the Varmas. Elsie watched him stare after the family, his body arrested, as if somewhere between ready to leap or stammer backward.

With the room empty, Jack barked at the waitresses, "Start breaking everything down." He shot a look at her behind the bar. Elsie turned away and busied herself with cleaning, scooping empty cups and lemon rinds into the trash can. *Asshole,* she thought, but worry rose in her chest like yeast in warm water. Those arms seemed so big around the bride, and they hooked themselves around her shoulders quickly, with no more effort than breathing.

Elsie didn't bother to count her tips and balled them into her pocket. On impulse, she took one of the unopened bottles of whiskey and stuffed it into her purse. This party was shit, and the host hadn't even bothered to tip her. The parking lot was emptying out. She was going home alone. The scales had to be balanced somehow.

With the bar clean and the empties in the garbage, Elsie

watched Jack maneuver through the dining room. Normally he and the waitresses went from table to table to finish up faster, but Jack's hunched shoulders said he worked alone, and the girls cleared tables on the other side of the room. Finally he shouted at them, "Just leave it! I'll take care of it myself." The two girls happily abandoned their tasks and said nothing as Jack slapped their wages into their open hands. Jack turned to Elsie across the room and held the cash from Ramesh, the money he'd given Jack to settle up at the end of the night. "Come get your money," he said, not trying to hide the disdain in his voice.

Elsie sucked in a hot breath and paced over to Jack in the center of the room. Her shoes squeaked across the tile, one hand on her hip and the other reaching for the twenties in his. When she touched the money, Jack waited a beat before releasing, her hand jerking back when he let go. "Go home," he said, and turned away to stack the chairs.

Elsie considered leaving with the waitresses. Her station was clean and the ice would melt in the sink. The booze was wearing off. The money was in her hand.

"Why you being so nice all of a sudden?" she said to his bending back. Jack stamped the chairs down, one on top of the next, punching down hard on the pleather cushions. Metal chair legs banged against one another.

She tucked the money into her back pocket and went around the table, grabbing a chair and offering it for the stack. "Here, let me help you."

"Just go home. You've done enough." Jack didn't look at her. He walked around her to grab another chair. "We're done early. You got what you wanted."

Elsie sneered and let the chair in her hands clang noisily

against the floor. "Don't you know when someone's trying to help you—"

"I don't need your help." Jack jammed the chair onto his stack hard, the clash of metal on metal echoing through the empty dining room. Elsie watched his shoulders rise and fall along with his breath. It took her a second to register her own breathing, shallow and stunted.

"What was I supposed to do with her?"

He waved her off and turned his attention back to the stack, jamming another chair on top with enough force that the whole structure teetered on two legs. Elsie grabbed the jutting chair legs on the opposite side. They pushed the stack upright, all four legs of the bottom chair jolting against the floor, and once the stack was balanced, they looked at each other. The stack was nearly as tall as Jack, and Elsie stood on the balls of her feet to meet his gaze.

Jack looked past her out the windows—the cars and the potholes were bathed in electric orange light, and a moth circled around the lamppost. He stepped back and planted his hands on his hips, trying to control the breaths clawing at his lungs.

"Ramesh was going to let me run the San Lorenzo restaurant if everything went well tonight." He pressed his palms over his closed eyes, then let his hands push across the crown of his head and move to the back of his neck. "I did it right, everything." Jack could hear the anger edging into his voice. The night before, he had watched Ramesh turn his gold ring around his pinkie as they went over the schedule for the wedding party. "I'm trusting you with tomorrow, Jagdish," Ramesh had said as he pulled his jacket on, the keys to the restaurant jingling in his hands. Tonight was supposed to be the night Jack proved himself, when all the sweat from washing dishes and busing tables would finally be behind him for good. After tonight, when he wrote to Sati about his management position, his importance to the company and his impatience to bring the family over, he could write with ease, not dread. After tonight every lie in every letter, past and future, would magically become true.

Elsie shifted from foot to foot, trying to find something to say. "It wasn't too bad, considering..." Her voice trailed off, and Jack turned back to the chairs, placing another chair on top. "You did a good job. You pulled off tonight without a hitch."

"Without what?"

"A hitch. It means everything went the way it was supposed to. You did it," Elsie said, but then smiled as she corrected herself. "It's not your fault she came up to the bar." She hoped Jack would smile with her, but he didn't. "I'm sorry," she said, her throat dry. "I've always been good at ruining things."

Jack snorted and shook his head. Quiet had settled on the restaurant. The cooks had shut down the kitchen after serving the dinner and had gone back to the house, and Lorena and Chinta were gone as soon as they were paid. The bay lights blinked beyond the windows like Morse code, electrical impulses, English, Sati's curled script across the page: letters, signals Jack pretended to understand.

Elsie let go of the stack and went up to the platform, then slumped into one of the chairs. She needed water and fresh air, or Manuel, or more whiskey, she couldn't decide. Kicking her legs out to stretch, her heel grazed over what felt like a rock, and she looked down to see the bride's gold jewelry tucked behind the chair's clawed foot. On picking up the swaddle of chains and glimmering jewels, their lightness surprised her. The bangles and the chain and bracelets were made of tin, the bells and golden balls plastic.

Elsie let out a pained laugh. "Shit, Jack! They're fakes!" They were nice knockoffs: Elsie couldn't tell the jewels weren't real until she had them in her hands, felt their weightlessness, the lack of substance. "Costume jewelry. No wonder she was pissed."

Working the jewelry in her hands, she listened to the hollow clack of the golden balls. She imagined the bride in a bedroom, afraid to touch anything in her new house as absolutely nothing was hers. Her future husband appeared, open box in hand, and the bride's eyes must have sparkled when she saw the gold and delicate chains. How heavy her heart must have felt once she took them up and put them on.

Jack took a few weary steps to the platform and collapsed into the empty chair next to Elsie. She held the metal jewels out to him, and he took a piece of the chain and strung it out to look at the links under the light.

"Is she going to be okay?" Elsie's voice was barely more than a whisper.

Jack didn't want to talk about the bride—she was a jab in his back that was cutting at the bone. The girl was probably tricked with letters promising far more than they would deliver; he still had the letters from Ramesh that promised a good job, a chance to bring Sati and Gupti to California.

"Don't worry about her," Jack said, his voice not as strong as he would have liked. "Everybody wants to get away, and they do what they must. She's no different." He dropped the chain down onto the pile of fake gold in Elsie's hands.

She slipped the bangles on and began threading the chains through her fingers like string. "You know what we need?"

He turned to her, his eyes tired. "What do we need?"

"Drinks," Elsie said, and she stood, carrying the jewels with her as she went back to the bar. Jack watched her find his cup behind the counter, then she grabbed the bride's drink from the bar top, which had not been touched since she had set it there. The drinks in one hand and the jewels in the other, her pace quickened across the floor, and she held the cups before him.

Jack shook his head. "I don't drink."

"You're a bad liar, Cook's Special," she said, pushing the plastic cups at him. He relented, pinched the lip of his cup and lifted it from her grasp. She watched him as he sniffed the drink, her smile flickering as he recoiled from the smell of the alcohol. The chains clinked as she took her seat. She held up the bride's drink, the amber swishing gently. Jack touched his cup against hers. They drank slowly.

"It's not bad luck to finish someone else's drink?" Jack asked after a moment.

Elsie shrugged and held the cup in the path of the spotlight above them, as if examining it. "Well, this is really good whiskey. Taste it. So smooth. It would be a waste to toss it." She swirled the whiskey in the cup, the funnel widening with the quickness of her wrist. A pair of low beams flashed through the window across the room, and Elsie sat up straight, her eyes following the path of light. It was only a minivan pulling out of the parking lot. She bit her bottom lip and leaned back. If only luck were transferable, a matter of drinking out of some lucky person's cup and inheriting their fate. What does Manuel's girl drink? Sparkling wine from a crystal flute? Soda straight from the can? Horchata, sangria, tequila, Slice—what does it matter? Her cup is full and sweet and sits besides Manuel's.

"If Ramesh gives you shit about tonight, just blame me," Elsie said after a while. "Tell Ramesh I brought the whole event down. Tell him that you tried to stop us both, but there was no reasoning with us." She laughed and swirled her drink, watched the vortex draw down to the bottom of the cup. "Tell him we were swigging straight from the bottle!" The laughter felt good, but it settled in her like cheap booze, sour on the way down and bitter in the stomach. The only reason she held on to the job at DiRaji's was because of Manuel: him coming to pick her up after these gigs was the only part of their relationship that didn't feel outright illicit. Usually, they met at the Berkeley marina or he would call her when he had the tattoo parlor to himself. But at DiRaji's, he was her man. He always touched her hand when she placed a drink before him. He stood behind her in the empty restaurant and lightly bit at her neck while she counted out her tips. He drove her home and laid her down in her bed, then stayed all night as if it was their place, as if what they had was real. Elsie dropped the jewels in her lap. "I think I'm quitting anyway."

"Why you leaving?" Jack looked at her, studying the silhouette of her profile against the light from the kitchen. Her eyelashes curled up like cups, like the curls he imagined sprouting behind Gupti's ears.

"I got a job at the VFW. It's full time. May as well," Elsie said, her voice low. "I've been here longer than everyone. Even you. Something's wrong with that." She forced out a chuckle and took another drink.

Jack looked away, a flush of heat rising up from his neck to his face. Two years was an eternity, but it was also a blink of an eye, the time passing effortlessly. When he left Delhi, Sati was just beginning to show, her breasts swelling and her middle widening. *You will never know I was gone,* he had whispered to her belly before boarding the bus to the airport. In the time Jack spent serving plates and mopping floors, Gupti grew. In the last letter, Sati said Gupti was learning to run, that his new favorite thing was to chase the goats in the courtyard. Jack tried to imagine holding the boy's body in his hands, his rib cage a little barrel, and Jack's own chest tightened. All he could see was Gupti from Sati's last set of pictures, hanging motionless from the branch of a mango tree, his eyes looking away from the shuttering lens, his image as flat in Jack's mind as the picture itself. When he could finally bring them over—Jack didn't want to think of when that would be anymore—Sati would have to point him out to their son, introduce them like strangers.

Jack tipped his cup back, then coughed with the flood of bitter alcohol in the back of his mouth. "So you're leaving me here?"

"Buck up, Jackie Boy. I'll come visit you." Elsie gently pushed at his arm, and Jack let himself be pushed across the chair.

He thought about Ramesh's cheap suit and greasy smile. He thought of the nighttime walk to the house with Assam snoring and Emilio and Santo playing cards by the glow of a muted television, the cot that waited to shuffle him to a light and short sleep. The smell of the whiskey reared and sought him out.

"This place is awful, isn't it?" Jack laughed, his cup nearly empty.

Elsie nodded. "Hasn't changed in years." She pointed to the fleur-de-lis bordering that went all around the walls of the restaurant. "They put that wallpaper up right after my first job here. Look how it's coming off." She took another drink and marveled at the rubbery warmth working its way through her body.

"Smells like soap. Or, what is it called...?" Jack looked to Elsie, who sniffed the air, then nodded in agreement.

"Stinks of oil and garlic, too. Cheap beer and curry and sweat." Her face twisted, and she took another drink.

"Bad curry." Jack finally laughed. "The food here, no good. Just the bread is good. My wife...at home, the food is much better." He finished the drink, a sigh sputtering out of him as he let the empty cup hang at his side. Elsie reached out, took his wrist in her hand, and poured some of the bride's drink into his cup. Her hand was warm, her fingers smooth and soft around his wrist. They held their cups and sat, their bellies warm and their heads light.

"You're married?"

He nodded. Only Emilio and Santo knew about Sati, having seen him shuffle through those letters, their eyes scanning over the pictures much like his own with a removed, reserved interest.

"You never told me. You're such a mystery." She clacked the balls together. His eyes were stuck on the windows. "What's her name?"

He sighed as he said it. "Sati." A moment ago he had wanted Elsie out of his sight. Before that, he had wanted her to laugh with him, make the time pass a little more lightly. Some nights, he wanted her in bed with him. Now just looking at her felt shameful. It was easy. He could see her, sometimes feel her body slide past his and remember how a woman's touch could soar through him. It was easier to lust after Elsie or Chinta or any of the other women around him instead of longing for Sati, with so much land and sea and space now between them.

She smiled and drank again. "I know she misses you."

He nodded but said nothing. She wanted to press him, cajole

him out of that look of locked, stunted anticipation. She looked away as she recognized that look on her own face, when she would sit in her car or on her bed or at the bar, waiting for her phone to ring, waiting for his voice to say, "Yes, I'm free. Come see me," in the way that she dreamed, the way that she knew now she would never get.

Above them, the tear in the bordering finally lost its last bit of resolve. The bordering gave way in slight sticky creaks, the weight of old paper and plaster dragging away from the wall. The pair looked up and saw the border falling, its tattered end hanging just over their heads.

"That's the saddest thing I've seen all night," Elsie said. In the shafts of light, little speckles of dust and paint spun and floated down, then disappeared in the darker folds of the room. "Feels like we've been here a thousand years," Elsie murmured, looking into her cup.

Jack looked up at the curl of bordering, remembered how many times he had retacked and reglued to keep those pieces together. Old oak sat on his tongue. "Because we have been."

Elsie stretched out in the chair, her arms and legs feeling like warm plastic. "We should just burn this place down." She giggled. "Purification through fire. I've got matches somewhere."

Jack rolled his head against the brocade of the chair and felt the thick stitching itch through the back of his shirt. He dug in his back packet. "I have a lighter."

Her dark lips broke into a smile. "Let's blame Assam. He smokes in the back all the time."

Jack nodded, wishing that his cup was bottomless. "He dropped his cigarette on the way out…Or maybe the host. He started it." Jack laughed with her. He snapped the lighter wheel.

Sparks jumped. Jack held the flame between them, and they watched it for a moment. His eyes stayed on the lighter in his hands, and Elsie thought his eyes looked so heavy, like stones at the bottom of a river. The little flame lit up Elsie's face, her cheeks and eyes aglow. The light undulated around them like waves, bright and strong under the dim chandeliers. The shadows of their bodies wavered in and out like ripples on the surface of water. The flame pulsed out from the platform, the light casting faintly across the room, but far, nonetheless.

PRINTS

EVERY WEDNESDAY DURING the fall of my first year at Carson Elementary and my first year in the states, Officer Hoenig came to my third-grade classroom before lunch. He had a thick mustache and big arms and sunglasses like mirrors that were always folded into his front shirt pocket. Our teacher called him Officer H, and he talked to us about saying no to drugs and never talking to strangers. He said to hold hands when crossing the street and to call an adult if we ever saw a gun. He said that we should never lie to our parents, to our teachers, to him, or to any of the police. "Lies hurt people," he said, his mustache twitching like the tail of a squirrel. "If you tell lies, people don't trust you."

One Wednesday he went around the room and asked the whole class what city each of us was born in. He went up and down each row and smiled at each response: San Leandro, Oakland, Stockton, San Leandro, Berkeley. Jo Beth Alvarez said she was born on East Fourteenth, and Jimmy Rosado cracked, "You were born on the street?" and everyone laughed, even Officer H. We all knew Ross Jackson was born in Texas by how he talked, and Officer H smiled and asked what he liked best about California. Ross Jackson said, "Nothing. I miss my old house." Officer

H smiled that same smile. "Texas sure is far from here," he said, and continued down the row.

His finger was working its way toward me, and I rehearsed in my head: *San Francisco, San Francisco, San Francisco.* The first thing Inay told me and my sister Carina about school was to always listen to the teacher, and the second was to never say that we were born in Manila. The first morning of school, she walked me to the school a few blocks from our house. Everywhere, the tree leaves were turning yellow and orange on their branches, sap all over the trunks. On the entrance steps, she adjusted my collar, then pulled a bit of string loose from the hem of my shirt and balled the blue thread between her fingers. She asked me again, "You know the story, right? If anyone asks, what will you say?" I told her I knew, and she smoothed my cowlick down from the crown of my head.

Officer H's hairy finger found me beside Alexandra Jacobs, who spoke first—"I was born in Los Angeles, Officer H!"—her dimples deep in her cheeks. His finger stayed on me. "How about you, little man?" I had been thinking, *San, San, San,* the whole time, but my lips still pressed into a *mmmmaaan* despite themselves. Officer H's finger twitched when my *mmmmm*-mouth parted into another shape entirely. My tongue slipped against my teeth into an *sssss,* sputtering the words out. Officer H didn't quite smile at my slow "San Francisco," and I waited for him to tell me it was wrong to lie, that he could see right through me. My toes curled inside my shoes, and I stared at his finger, everything blurring behind it. I was sure his eyes were bearing down on me hard, but then his finger had traveled behind me and arrived at Ms. Carabello, our teacher, who said she was born in New York City. Everyone oohed and aahed that she was born so far away. My neck felt tight, like a hot palm against my skull, and I shook my shoulders, felt my throat rise and my voice find its place among the rest of the class.

THE STORY WAS simple enough: In 1984, my parents came to San Francisco to live with my dad's great-aunt Silva, who had a basement room for them to rent. In the story, they're newlyweds, in love. Inay worked at a hospital processing medical reports, and Itay worked for a freight transport company. They worked hard. Inay was certified as a public accountant, and Itay became a manager at the company. That part of the story is true, as far as I know. They prospered, earned enough to send kitchen appliances and clothes and tapes of Bon Jovi and The Police back to the family. They could take Carina and me to Manila to visit. That explains the pictures of us as kids climbing the avocado trees in Manila—from vacations, they could say, family reunions, brief visits back. It is a simple story, one that covers the basics in broad strokes, no elaboration necessary. That was the point when I was young, having a story simple enough that I could tell it with a straight face, even if fear was clawing its way up my throat, the truth ready to fall out of my mouth.

I REMEMBER THE fog the most. Every day, sometimes all day, it was foggy and the air was always full of cold water. I wore three shirts and my jacket and a fuzzy brown hat to stay warm in Aunt Silva's sliver of a backyard, and Carina barely went farther than the back porch to avoid the shivering cold.

Aunt Silva lived on the top floor with her two grown sons. I barely saw them at all—they were never around when we were there. We all stayed down in the basement. Carina and I slept next to each other, her ear brushing my ankles, and on cold nights, her feet nestling against my ribs. Inay and Itay had a proper bed behind the staircase, and at first, they always stayed back there together, one of them coming home late when the other rose early, but always together back there behind the stairs where we would not see them.

Aunt Silva was good for some things—she told us stories about Inay and Itay back home, how when Inay was a little girl, she saw ghosts in the trees and once went running through a neighbor's house screaming that an old man that no one could see was chasing her. My favorite stories were about Itay, how he wore bell-bottoms and had his black hair permed into a bouffant shell on his head.

Those first few months Aunt Silva watched us a lot, and she was nothing like Lala Thea, who took care of Carina and me in Manila while our parents were setting up shop in California. Lala treated us like her own children; we were another chore to Aunt Silva, who washed her absent sons' laundry and complained about the takeout boxes they stacked in the refrigerator and never ate. "I'm no maid to you," she growled when picking up our toys off the basement steps. She was both old and ageless, her skin always tight around her eyes and mouth. She liked Carina, who was five and still young enough to be cute on command, but she was done with me after those first few afternoons, especially after I started playing with the wall phone one day, trying to call Lala Thea, but instead connecting to an office in New Jersey. She wasn't there, but there was music playing through the receiver, and I listened for a while until I got bored and left the phone on the kitchen table. When the phone bill came, the new rule was not to touch anything upstairs unless Aunt Silva or Inay or Itay put it in our hands. In practice, the rule meant, *Be like the breeze against a window—invisible.*

MY FAVORITE THING when we first came to the states was driving—we didn't have a car back home. We took a taxi if we were going across the city, or if we were spending a day at the beach, but those trips were rare. When Inay first brought us over to San Francisco, we walked just about everywhere. Mostly we went to school or stayed at home and tried to avoid Aunt Silva, but on the days when no one could watch Carina and me, our dad had to take us to work with him in Oakland Chinatown. They were the lucky days. Carina and I would run to the car, excited for the engine revving and the radio crackling with rock and roll.

Crossing the Bay Bridge, the tires thumping over each divot and the water whitecapping below us, I never wanted to actually arrive at the office. If I had my way, we would have gone without stopping, just slowing down for a better look or speeding up to pass by. I liked the feeling of the car moving, how at sixty miles an hour, I was floating. It was fun, knowing how fast the ground was traveling underneath me.

On the bridge looking at the skyscrapers, we were suspended above a glimmering city, the sun gashing the western-facing windows and my eyes with white light. I liked the faraway view, the movements of the city in miniature—big rigs became matchbox cars, tall trees were shrubs, and people were barely visible, just black ants crawling in long lines. I tried to imagine Manila from that vantage point, but I saw only the courtyard of our complex, its cinder-block walls painted red and chalky with white dust. I saw the map of the mainland framed on the wall of Lala Thea's patio, our city marked with a red star. I couldn't imagine Manila's towers and clustered buildings from such a height, how I could pull far away enough to see something so big.

In Chinatown, through one-way streets with funny writing on the street signs, I remember Itay moving a chain-link gate to park in an alleyway. He marched Carina and me into a dim sum restaurant that had golden ducks and racks of brown ribs hanging in the window. The place smelled like fat and ginger; I always got water mouth as soon as we pushed through the glass doors. Usually, Itay sat us in the far back at a booth with cracked leather seats and green bamboo shoots painted on the nearby wall. "Behave until I get back," he said like clockwork, and disappeared up a staircase tucked in the back of the restaurant lobby.

At home, if left to ourselves, Carina and I would stay in the basement and play and fight and go back to playing. But at the restaurant, we knew to sit quietly and draw with crayons on paper placemats and eat the chicken wings brought to us by the bucktoothed waitress. Her name was something Chinese, but her name tag read Leah, and she liked to sit with us when there were no other customers to pay attention to. She watched us draw and brought us Cokes, and she sometimes dotted a paper napkin into a water glass to wipe sweet and sour sauce off Carina's face. She grinned when she could grab hold of our chins and scrub, and she always studied our drawings, my fighter jets and astronaut stick men and Carina's Mickey Mouse waving on the beach. She would wink at Itay when he came down the stairs into the restaurant dining room and say, "Such beautiful children." She would look up at him and breathe in deep, working one of her gold bracelets around her wrist.

Itay gave his soft chuckle—the one he gave to Aunt Silva when she complained about us kids fighting or to Inay when she asked him where he had been the night before—and then grabbed the top of my head and pushed my hair around. He looked at her and then at me. "Very well behaved."

"SHOW ME," HE said, his chin hovering over my shoulder. I was at his desk downstairs, tracing an airplane from a magazine. I helped myself to some of Itay's thin, wispy sheets that were under a box filled with thick white paper. It's funny. I always thought he was an artist, since his fingers were always covered with ink or lead. I thought that for a long time, even though I never saw a painting or a drawing, nothing that was his. It must've been Aunt Silva, who'd mutter at Carina and me about "your father, the artist" while my parents fought quietly in their corner of the basement.

Itay stood behind me, almost blocking the lamplight with his shoulders. "Your granddad flew planes like these," Itay said. I relaxed. I wasn't in trouble.

I pulled the paper up, and he took it. The wings of the plane and the body were traced perfectly straight, and the angle of the propeller matched up exactly to the picture. Itay held the tracing paper over the magazine, his eyes bearing down on the page. He smiled at my work. I wanted to know what he was looking for, what he could see beyond the lines.

"Good job, Gardo," he said, then pulled a tack from the desk drawer and pinned my biplane to the wall. I gripped the pencil in my hand a little tighter.

He put a blank sheet in front of me. "Write your name." I wrote Edgardo Villanueva in my standard block print. "Write it again in cursive," he said. I did. Then he took the pencil from my hand and scribbled out a name, John Roberts.

"Who's John Roberts?" I asked, and Itay said, "No one. This is just for practice." Then he put the tracing paper on top, so that the name on the page underneath looked like a fence in a snowstorm.

"Draw the name like you drew the plane."

It was harder, with the loops and the curl attached to the straight back of the *r*, and the print was a bit jagged, but I did it. After a few more tries, he pulled back the tracing paper.

"Look where the ink gets lighter." He pointed to the light sweep between the *o* and the *h*, the *b* and the *e*. "Follow the ink," he said. I did. He pulled the tracing paper up and told me to do it again, until I had a whole column of John Roberts running down the page like a waterfall. Itay took that page and placed it facedown, then put a clean piece of paper in front of me. He told me to write the name again without tracing, just by looking.

I thought about it. I wanted to practice one more time.

"Don't think about it too much. Just do it like before," Itay said.

I did like he told me—I let my palm relax, eased the pen away from the page, then dipped back and scrawled. He held up the original to my print of it. He smiled.

"You're a natural, son."

"A natural what?"

"Artist, like me." He winked. "Artists can become other people. Like you, just now—you practice being John Roberts on this page, and then presto!" He held my John Roberts' print in front of me. "Your hand knows John Roberts so much that your hand is John Roberts' hand. You see?"

I didn't, but I nodded. The only time my dad ever got excited was when he played mah-jongg in the basement with Aunt Silva and the Pablo brothers. I'd never seen him not force a smile when he was with me, until now.

"You can be anyone you want. Fun, huh?"

"So there is a John Roberts," I said. I tried to imagine what John Roberts looked like. It seemed like a common name. It made me think of a man in a suit and hat in front of a green lawn. It seemed like a name for someone on TV.

"There's a John Roberts now," he said. "You made him real."

AFTER A YEAR, one of Aunt Silva's sons cleared out his bedroom and was not spoken of again, and so Carina and I were moved upstairs. Two little beds made an *L* against the wall, and we would sometimes sleep with our toes touching or with the wisps of her black hair grazing mine. Sometimes at night, Carina would wake me up. She had nightmares about getting sent back. I could hear her talking in her sleep. She'd giggle or murmur in Tagalog, but sometimes she would say no in English, no, no, no, and then she'd kind of shake herself awake. She'd poke me and say my name, "Gardo, Kuya Gardo." I'd let her crawl over and get under the blankets with me. She had dreams of going to jail, that the police had taken our parents away. She would fold her arms and wriggle in bed, and complain that her stomach hurt no matter what she ate.

I'd grab the stuffed Mickey off the floor and make it talk like our Lala Thea used to do—she had a bear with yellow fur that she would hold up before her face, and she would drop her voice and wiggle the bear's arms and head with her fingers. Anything the bear said, we believed. Carina lost that bear on the flight from Manila to Honolulu, but Itay brought a Mickey Mouse with big ears and gloved hands for us when we touched down in San Francisco. At night when Carina got scared, I held Mickey in front of my face like Lala would.

"What's wrong, ding dong?"

Carina pushed her black hair behind her ear and whispered, "Sometimes I have bad dreams, Mickey. I hear sirens. Like on TV. Police come and take people away."

I crinkled Mickey's body, made him scratch his ear in thought. "Now, ding dong, a dream can't hurt you. It's all in your ulo, see?" I pushed Mickey's arm toward her forehead, and she held back a laugh. "You and big brother know the story, right?"

Carina nodded her head up and down, her eyes stuck on the black beads sewn on Mickey's face.

"What do you say if someone asks?"

I had trained her with this answer, and she always said it with force: "Nothing."

"Well then," Mickey said, and jumped on her shoulder. "You're too smart to worry." I scrunched up Mickey's body and pecked her cheeks with his fuzzy nose. Lala called them bear kisses in Manila, and now, in San Francisco, they were Mickey kisses. "No more bad dreams, no more." Carina giggled, and she pulled his plush body tight against her chest.

Some nights we talked about going to the market outside the complex with Lala, who bought us sugared mango and empanadas if we pleaded long enough. She took us with her wherever she went and always kissed us good night. Before we came here, Inay was a vision, a picture on the wall and a voice on the phone, but Lala was soft cotton dresses and bare feet that stayed clean, warm towels after cold bucket baths. It seemed like a world away from here, where Inay watched us eat dinner while she went over tax papers, nodding absently at whatever we said.

The last time Inay had come to the complex, I was excited because she said we were going to visit San Francisco. I had told Lala, "I'm going on vacation! Why can't you come with us?" At seven, I was better at evoking tears than calming them. I didn't know why she was sad or how to make her stop crying. It wasn't until we were on the plane that Inay told us we were going to our new house, that we were not coming back, not for a long time. Carina fidgeted as Inay snapped the seat belt across her lap. How long, I wanted to know. Inay wouldn't answer me, just kept saying, "You will love California, anak. Trust me. You'll love it." I thought of Lala waving from the gate of the complex, how I hadn't hugged her. I hadn't said good-bye, just waved and ran to the taxi. I felt my stomach drop as the plane surged upward, and I pressed my face against the double-paned window, catching the green edge of the island just before it disappeared from view. The island evaporated in the fog, but I kept looking, thinking maybe Lala could see the plane from the complex and see me through the window, looking for her.

Some nights I could talk about Manila. Carina liked to remember. What kind of tree was that in the complex, the one with the fuzzy green fruit? What was the name of that neighbor lady next door, the one who always sang along to the operas on the radio? Do you remember when the Guintos got a TV, and we had to give them pesos to watch cartoons?

But other nights, I would hear Carina moving, and I would lie still as a stone. She would reach from her bed to mine and poke at my foot or my knee, and I would pretend to be asleep, my eyes shut tight. I wouldn't move or swallow, would hardly breathe until she balled herself under her blankets and turned toward the wall.

ITAY'S OFFICE IN Chinatown was smaller than my and Carina's room, but it had a closet filled with boxes and another door behind it with locks. When I was little, I loved that one little door in the closet: the secret door leading to an unknown room in a mystery building, where people floated through the hallways soundlessly and doors never seemed to open. How many ways could one get in, get lost, escape?

I couldn't have been there more than a few times as a kid, but I remember the place well: up the linoleum stairs, fourth whitewashed door to the right, green carpet gone brown from too much time. Inside, brown boxes were stacked high against the walls. Some lids were loose, while others were sealed with silver tape. A desk pushed against the window looked out onto the third floor of another building with the same pale brick and crackled bits of paper stuck in the walls. A moss green typewriter squatted on the floor beside the desk, several of its keys jabbing into the air. Rolls of plastic laminate as tall as me leaned against the corners of the room.

The few times he took me there, I always knew better than to ask why we'd stopped or what was in the boxes or locked drawers. I knew better than to ask about most things, like why he had been staying away from the house and why Inay slept upstairs in Aunt Silva's living room when he was home. By that time, I learned what questions to keep to myself.

I remember Itay riffling through the desk, unlocking drawers. His hands full of papers, he turned to a card table in the corner and sat down. I hovered behind, watching him arrange the papers in a rough pile.

"What are you making?" I asked. He was fitting a razor on the end of a pen. He hunched his shoulders over the sheets in front of him and told me to go to the desk and draw him a picture. I watched his arms work from behind, how the movements of his hands showed themselves in his back, in the slight shake of the metal folding chair beneath him.

I looked for a blank sheet of paper and a pen on the desk. The top and bottom drawers wouldn't give. Under a pile of papers and an adding machine, I found some plain white paper, but I drew only lines and circles. I wrote my name over and over in fat block letters because I had no subject to draw but my father. I wanted to draw his hands, but he moved too quickly for me to capture them.

I liked it when he would disappear down the hall. I'd listen for his footsteps or a door swinging open, but once the door was closed behind him, it was as if he vanished. I'd wait a beat, sure he'd materialize back just as quickly. When I felt brave enough, I would explore.

At the desk, I'd feel for unlocked drawers. Once one gave, and I found glass bottles filled with liquid—red, green, blue, and more than any other color, black that ran thick and thin against the glass. On the card table, stacks of thick colored paper were gathered in heaps. Each pile had different colors, and some had different textures, fibrous or smooth like plastic. I leafed through the pages. A scratch from my fingernail notched a streak through a loop of translucent rainbows embossed over a blue page, and I took it and put it at the bottom of the stack.

In a green metal box stuck next to the mystery door, I found little leather books from what seemed like every country—lime green Argentina, high-noon blue Italy, navy blue United States, chocolate brown Jordan, fire-engine red Taiwan. Some were blank, but others were just old. The photos were black-and-white, and the pages were just pages, no series of lines along the borders or special stamps that touched both name and photo. Looking at the pictures inside, I saw some had the same names as the kids I went to school with, which fascinated me, as if they were all family: John Michael Hall (hair greased and drawn tight across his brow), Elizabeth Delancey Stuart (thin lips with a high-necked blouse), Timothy Eladio Caires (the cheeks ruddy, the eyes black), Lyle Eric Nielson (eyes clear as glass, looking slightly away from the camera lens). I flipped through them until the names and faces began to bleed together.

Against the wall, there was a tall roll of laminate, almost bigger than me and cool against my cheek. Once, I peeled back a corner from one of the rolls. The edge of my fingerprint stood out clear as day when I tugged it from the sticky side. I went back to the desk, where a magnifying glass curved its long neck toward the window. I flipped the light switch on at its base and looked at the ridges of my fingers. In school we were learning about topography, how the thickness and color of the lines meant streets or highways or country roads. The ridges of my fingerprint reminded me of the bunched loops of a mountain. The lines on my palm curved like rivers.

No matter how alert I was, no matter how carefully I listened for his steps, he'd always catch me hunched in a box or in midleap away from it. "You don't listen, do you?" he would usually say, and swivel me toward the door, his hand pressed between my shoulder blades. Through the door, down the stairs, out of the restaurant, and into the world, our footsteps sounded so loud.

AT SCHOOL, I am Eddie. On my school ID, I am Edgar Villanueva, and my picture isn't grainy enough to hide the acne on my cheeks. On papers I write only my last name with the capital V like a dagger coming down. To the assistant vice principal, I am Mr. Vil-la-nu-va. On the street, I am Eddie. "Go, Chinaman," I have heard more than once when I'm skateboarding down a sloping street. In the malls, I am Suspect, shadowed by security guards. To Carina's boyfriends, I am Scary Gary. To the neighbors, I am one of Aunt Silva's sons or maybe a nephew (the eyes and the years play tricks), but probably trouble, just like the other two. To girls, I am whatever name they go with, and if they hear the other names I am called, they look at me like I'm playing a trick on them. In the end, I always am. On the back of family photos, I am Edgardo Junior. At home, Inay calls me anak and only that. She says my name only when speaking about me to someone else. Itay calls me son when he is proud of me and has no name for me when he is angry. Carina calls me Eddie when we're at school, Gardo in front of family, and kuya—brother—when we are alone.

MY PARENTS STILL talked, just not in front of Carina or me. I was about to graduate, and I'd been accepted at Holy Names across the bay. It was the paperwork that made me nervous. I never showed any forms to go to school before, but now I needed a social security card and a birth certificate. Like everything in my life, both parents jockeyed about who would do what while I twisted in the wind. I figured between the two of them, they had my whole paper life manufactured—instead, the most official documents with my name on them that either of them could drum up were my report cards and a TB test from ninth grade. I only began to give a shit when I turned seventeen and was a stone's throw away from getting my driver's license.

Itay drove up to the house, but he didn't get out of the car. He honked four times, and I went out to the street to meet him. I slid into the passenger side.

"Let me get a look at you," he said, then pushed my shoulder back and grabbed my chin to look at my face. "When are you cutting those things off your head?"

"The ladies love the dreads, man," I said, waving away his fingers that pulled at one of my locks.

"You smell like smoke," he muttered, but he didn't seem too upset about it. It had been three months since the last time we'd seen each other, and our visits before that had been sporadic and brief. Work was our common excuse.

"I'm proud of you, anak. To be accepted, well..." He didn't finish, and I nodded, deciding to take his words at face value. His shoulders hunched as he fished in his wool coat and pulled out an envelope with aerogram stamps. He held it out for me to grab.

"Yours?" I asked.

"No. I don't do those anymore. But I know a guy in Piedmont. Owed me a favor," my dad said, squinting at me. At least he didn't bother to lie. From the corner of my eye I saw the curtain in our front window move then rest. When I took it, he said, "Give it to your mom. She knows what to do with it." He didn't call her Inay anymore, and neither did I, really.

He asked how Carina was. I didn't tell him about her old boyfriend who kept calling the house threatening to kill her. He asked if we had enough money, and I said yes to that, too, but that a twenty always helps. He didn't reach for his wallet, and I rubbed my palm against the leather door handle, waiting for the right kind of silence to arise so that I could leave.

That night after dinner, Mom brought the ironing board out and set the envelope at the edge. Steam rose and caught her hair as she ran the iron quickly over the envelope's mouth. She came into the bright light of the kitchen and worked the envelope open with a razor blade. Her fingers were quick, and the glue seal was undamaged.

The certificate was thick between my fingers and had the same texture as wood that needed sanding. It felt like my prom announcement, with its embossed titles standing up under my fingers. The slightly dog-eared paper and the hospital stamp at the bottom looked appropriately weathered. She held the certificate up to the light and tapped her nail on the "County and State of Birth" box just below my name.

But it was not my name. It was Michael Eduardo Villanueva, all in computer-generated capital letters. The stamp looked official. The indent of the seal swooped over the first name entirely, and the circle curved shut. I held it up to see the watermark. I bent it, looking at the little swirls dancing in loops just like there were supposed to be. There was my last name, my birth date, Itay's name, and Inay's maiden name. On the page was what should be everything about my birth, and it was. But my name is Edgardo, not Michael, and I was not born in the county of San Francisco. The certificate said otherwise, and the stamp made it official. Even to the trained eye, it was a remarkably well-executed fraud.

"Why Michael?" I asked, looking at Michael Eduardo in bold type. Eduardo was the closest thing to my real name, Edgardo, and I rubbed my finger across the middle name, thinking the difference between *g* and *u* was huge, no matter how you looked at it.

She smacked my hand. "Don't muss it, anak. The ink's still fresh," she said, and inspected where my fingers had been.

I CAUGHT THE N-Judah to the DMV near Golden Gate Park—I cut out on school that day to take care of my license. I had done the practice test and driven around the neighborhood in my mom's Acura so many times, I felt like I didn't even need the license. I knew it all already. The park was lush and green, shaded from the tall trees. As I walked in, I felt a familiar twinge in my stomach, a thread of anxiety weaving its way through my muscles. I took a deep breath, took a number, sat, and waited.

The college and the DMV needed the same kinds of paperwork, which I thought was pretty funny. In a manila envelope, I had all the documents they said I would need to verify my identity and finalize my acceptance. I figured the DMV was a good test—if the birth certificate worked here, then I would never need to show it again. My nerves were rattling, and I did my best to breathe normally. After this, the license would be enough. No need for a story anymore. No more worrying. The license would be my proof.

While I took my test, the pen kept slipping between my sweaty fingers. There were officers floating around the facility, leaning against walls and resting their hands on their holsters. When I finished, a woman behind a flat-board cubicle went over my test with a red marker, and then said without enthusiasm that I had passed. She sent me to another line, where they would process my paperwork and take my picture.

I waited in a row of plastic orange chairs, fidgeting. I was glad to be alone. My mom would be double-checking the packet every few minutes and working a crease into the strap of her purse with her worrying hand. My dad wouldn't have come regardless. I moored myself in the corner and rolled my fingers against the plastic armrest, the ghost of my fingerprint appearing and disappearing with each press.

A man in a short-sleeved shirt and a tie that reached only midway down his thick waist appeared, and he called out "Michael" three times, and then he tried "Mr. Villanueva," and my ears burned as I stood up. I apologized. "I go by my middle name, sir," I said, almost stumbling over the words I had practiced. The packet in my hand felt slightly damp, and I reminded myself that all they needed was a quick glance, in this case maybe a photocopy, and that's it, I'm in. No one knows my name isn't Michael, I repeated in my head, no one suspects anything.

I placed my documents in the man's open hand. He opened the envelope and slid my father's handiwork in front of him. Just like when I was a kid practicing "San Francisco, San Francisco," I reminded myself that no one knows the real story but me. *No one knows,* I kept thinking. *No one knows.*

THE RAPOSAS

You don't even know the half of it. You know how the FBI got their foot in the door in the first place? It was because of them Raposa boys.

When Driesback opened up in '69, the only way in and out of the neighborhood was on East Eleventh. You know how the yard got that bottleneck entryway into the loading dock? The trucks would block it all day and all night trying to unload and get over to their next pickup at the Del Monte plant or the naval yards or the port. Damn logistical nightmare when you had more than two trucks trying to dock. The street's only big enough for one rig at a time, and they used to have drivers lined up two blocks deep just to unload. That's when Sherwood was running the yard, and he couldn't do much, since right across from the docks it's all residential. What was he going to do? Widen the street his own damn self?

Now Raposa and his boys, they lived right across from the docks in that white house with the pitched roof. Raposa had lived across from the docks forever and worked there before the Driesback outfit bought the dock from the Roswells. He and his three sons come up to Sherwood one day—this must have been summer of '70—and they tell him they got a notion for how to get the trucks in and out without blocking the whole street.

The old man would line up the trucks and wave them into the shipping yard, and his boys would load and unload. From how I heard it, Mr. Raposa was plenty convincing. Three sons big as bulls probably helped, but I tell you, Raposa was a charmer. Could make you think you weren't paying him for a service, but just tipping him for helping you out. Smooth as engine grease, and just as clean.

I don't know if Sherwood thought it could work or if he was just shit out of ideas, maybe just scared. But he let the Raposas start running the dock. The old man would motion the rigs along and order them to unload, and his sons were lumping shit on and off the trucks. Most of the truckers didn't mind—why lug pallets on or off yourself when there's someone right there offering to do it for you? For a little something, of course. Well, most of us didn't mind. Figured those were the breaks if we wanted to get our loads on and off as quick as we could.

Them Raposa boys had thick arms and thick heads, too. They were all right. They liked to throw their weight around when they had the chance. Those kind of guys. The oldest, Mario, I heard him tell this long-haul driver from Louisville that if he wanted to unload his own trailer, he could, but it might be hard to unload with broken fingers. Subtle as shit, but they kept things moving. Productivity was up—we had one of the best turnaround times of all the yards in Oakland. Management was giving plenty of overtime.

So everything's going fine for a while. I had just started driving, doing short hauls through the bay. I'd load up and head out to Salinas, Gilroy, up to the North Bay sometimes. The boys weren't all bad to me, but I made sure to stay on their good side. Their old man would be posted up right here in the morning, far end of the bar. Drank beer with tomato juice and Tabasco, and always called over any drivers he'd seen to come share a drink. Sometimes one of his boys was there, too. Back then, the Gato used to open at five in the morning just to catch the dockworkers and the drivers getting off night shift. Plus, the rounds were always cheap that early. Two-dollar pitchers until nine. Well, Raposa would let me get the first round, then he would call the barman over and say he would pick up the rest. He was all right—he knew how to take care of his folks.

So for a while everything was great. The oldest, Mario, and the middle one, I think his name was Frankie, they had everything running on clockwork. They were never on the books, but Sherwood paid them all, just the same. I mean, we were all getting taken care of somehow. It was kickback city when the yards were really moving back then, before the production plants started downsizing and moving inland. Wheels got greased, corners got cut. Loads fell off the back of the trucks all the time. It's the "all the time" part that gets you though. The gravy train gotta run out of track some time.

Some cross-country drivers got to complaining. It pissed them off. I guess I could see their end of things. I'd have been pissed off, too, if I had to pay some local lumpers to get my loads off quick. Raposa had everyone by the balls, too. Every driver was on a different schedule, and back then, we didn't have mandatory rest periods or pay for idle time. Everyone had to do what they had to do to make it on time to the next drop-off or pickup. The Raposa boys didn't mind stepping on toes and twisting arms if some drivers didn't want to play. There were always a lot of swinging dicks in the yard, and Mario liked to swing his.

This Swede named Gorman, he was an independent operator,

had his own rig. Took his dogs with him on runs, two big black Labs. Gorman was serious about his work. He had to be. All the man had was his rig and those dogs. Well, he and Mario went at it all the time. It was those dogs that started it. Gorman trained them to be loud and mean. Protection on the road. A mean-looking mutt could be more effective than a baseball bat that you had to dig out from under the seat. Those dogs would bark at Mario like he was the devil himself.

I remember the first time Gorman had his dogs with him in the rig, when Mario came up to wave him through, those labs started barking and Mario damn near shit himself. Turned white as powder! The whole yard was busting up, all the lumpers and the drivers in line, even Old Man Raposa was laughing. Mario got all pissed off, threatened to shoot those dogs if Gorman brought them around again. So Gorman went through the line, and Mario came up to get his unloading fee. Gorman tells him to get his money through the pay office like the real workers, then one of the dogs snaps its teeth, and Mario jumps the fuck back. And this is Mario, big talk, big mouth Mario, who shut the hell up real quick. Priceless.

Of course, after that, Mario made a point of pushing Gorman to the back of the line. All the lumpers slow-loaded him, sometimes dropped a few of the boxes that Gorman was delivering. Gorman got into it with someone just about every time he was at the docks. Couldn't be helped. Just about everything was being funneled through the West Oakland port. No avoiding the Raposas. I heard Gorman dropped the dime because he never had any more drop-offs at Driesback when investigators began popping up and snooping around. But then, it could have been anybody.

It wasn't all the Raposas, I don't think. There are a million ways to scrape some fat from the hog, and everyone was in on it somehow. Back then, there wasn't anyone to double-check the inventory against the paperwork. Some of the guys used to sell stuff right off the back of the rig, and there were plenty of people with money in their hands, ready to buy whatever was selling. It was gravy, but as soon as the feds came around, the t's got crossed and the i's got dotted. Raposa and his boys were just the face of it, right out in front on the street. Everyone was shitting a brick, from the Raposas on up to Sherwood and management. And the feds, they act like they don't need to be low-key. This one time, a little while after we started seeing them float around the docks, these two walked right up to my cab and flashed a badge. Didn't need no badge, since we all knew exactly who they were in those black suits. They asked about fee charges for loading and unloading. Who's doing your unloading? Who do you turn in your paperwork to? Are there independent workers? That's how they phrased it—independent workers. I kept my mouth shut. I wasn't going to be the one to give them anything to go on, and I didn't want to get pushed to the back of the line when all of the bullshit blew over.

I didn't see the arrests myself—it was my off day—but I heard the feds came in force. Arrested all the Raposas, Sherwood, too, and they took the management suits in for questioning. All of the suits were back the next day, but the Raposas were gone. Some jurisdiction loophole said that the Raposas were interfering with interstate commerce. Can you believe that? Who knows what they were really there for—feds were all over the place back then, starting trouble all over, keeping tabs on all kinds of people, I shit you not. Docks are a good place for trouble, though, and it stopped mattering what brought them around in the first place. At least back then there wasn't any doublespeak from the company—they fired Sherwood and banned the Raposas from the docks. They called all us short-haul drivers in and told us they were "restructuring." Management fired some personnel and changed the logo.

It took a while before everything started to die down. With so many eyes on the dock, there were no more scams on the line. Feds went after the higher-ups, and all they could shake loose was a few tax evasion charges for the pencil pushers in accounting. A few went to a cushy mid-security prison for a few months. They let Sherwood hang—he went to Santa Rita with Raposa and Mario. They got sent up for a merchandise scam Mario ran in the warehouses, boxing up clunker TVs and packaging them in brand-new boxes then sending them off to flea markets. He took the brunt of it and got more time than his old man. There were other charges, I don't remember what. Small shit, but that's how they get you, on the small stuff.

When Raposa and his oldest were inside, the middle one was in a traffic accident that summer that turned him into a vegetable. Don't know what happened to the youngest.

When he got out, the old man couldn't hang around the yard, so he stayed up on his stoop. I'd go have a brew with him when I got off shift, but around that time, I had put in my papers with Local 70. I was already pretty much out of Driesback by then. I got a warehouse job with Lucky's, and these days there isn't too much of a reason to come back out to East Eleventh. Except the Gato. The pitchers are still a deal in the morning, but you got to get here early.

Before I was out of there, I'd sometimes see the old man on

my way out. Raposa's house is still there, across from dock three. Stop and have a beer. Old man had a view of the whole operation from his front door, and he'd look at it like he had big plans. "It's just a matter of time," he'd say. He talked about the yard like it was his. "No one can make money off this dock without me," he'd say. Haven't seen him in years, but his house is still there. Must have been there at least a year ago. I could see a mountain of empties lined up on the old man's porch last time I drove past.

STUDIES IN
ENTROPIC BOTANY

Joanne

When my dad talked about his old neighborhood, he would always begin with, "Back when I was growing up, the families on my block could make a living, I mean a decent living." He'd say this, laying stress on the word *decent*. That rise in his throat over the word meant we'd come up by being *more* decent than those back on Sixty-seventh Avenue. It also had this obliviousness, as if our neighborhood close to the lake didn't have those *less* decent people. Even though we lived away from the thick of it in East Oakland, it was everywhere. When I was little and my mama was still around, she would shoo my sister Leslie and me past these men, all strung out, lying on park benches with their eyes red and their lips chapped like chipped wood. There was always news about crack in East Oakland on TV at night, and my dad would shake his head and get up to get a beer, taking his time so when he'd return to us in the living room, the next segment about traffic or sports would be under way.

My dad grew up in the villages on Sixty-seventh Avenue when it was a bustling place. All the men who worked at the ports and the frozen-food warehouses bought nice houses in the mid-sixties neighborhood: brick chimneys, slanted roofs, chain fences, square lawns. My dad worked as a driver for the canning plant in the indus-trial zone in West Oakland; he wore his Local 70 shirt under his work clothes every day and bought a remodeled Victorian across from Lake Merritt right before I was born. I grew up hearing my dad and my aunt always telling me and Leslie that we had gotten out of something bad—that's how they described it.

"You're lucky you're in a place where you can make some-thing of yourself. If you were coming from the villages, daugh-ter of mine, you'd have to work a lot harder to make it through," my dad told me whenever I complained about school or my homework. Then he'd start talking about hard work and dil-igence and gumption, how he worked all his life and worked hard still to make sure Leslie and I had what he called "a run-ning start." I hated it when he said those things to me, that somehow I was ahead of the game, that we were lucky. I didn't feel like it: our mom took off when I was six and Leslie was two, and I hated explaining that we didn't know where she was to teachers and neighbors and whoever else thought it was their business. I liked the kids at school who were bused in from East Oakland because they didn't think it was weird that my mom wasn't around or that I had to cook dinner for my sister and take care of the house.

My dad liked to think that everything was fine at our house by the lake, and I always managed to ruin it for him. I would giggle about the girls walking the streets at night, and he'd glare at me and say, "One day we'll talk about all that." At reunions jumping double-dutch with my cousins, we'd sing, "Crackhead, smackhead, dope-nose fathead, tell me how many hits you had? One, two, three, four…" My dad heard us, came across the back-yard, turned me by my shoulder, and sent the ropes flying out of my hands. He said I didn't know what I was talking about, and where'd I learn that crap, anyway? I told him that's what everyone sang on the playground because I was too young to know when to shut up.

I learned all kinds of things from Freddy and the other kids who were bused up to our school from the villages. Freddy and Edina and Brittany all knew the signs—spray paint on building sides, broken road signs, a car parked on the wrong side of the street—for all these things that my dad swore up and down didn't happen in our part of town. They could point at black and brown and white shoes hanging on telephone wires and tell what kind of drugs you could buy on which block. On the way from school to our house, over the hill and near the freeway on-ramp, there was an apartment building that always had people standing in front, rain or shine. My friend Freddy told me one day when we were going to my house after school that they were lookouts. "They watch for cops and keep the loud crackheads in line," Freddy said, like it was plain as day and funny that I didn't just *know*.

There was a bag lady that stayed in one spot in the park that I could see from my bedroom window—I had always thought that she just loved the shade of this one tree that was always full of birds. Edina and Brittany had come over to my house, and I showed them that sweet old lady. They laughed and pointed to a little dirt path into the bushes, just beyond where the bag lady was camped. I heard voices and saw a lighter flash beyond the wall of leaves.

Most of the time we had fun. We played tag by the lake and dunked our arms in the fountains for change to buy ice cream. Brittany and Freddy told me about block parties where music played all night, and I would imagine the scene—our neighborhood was full of old people who complained if someone had their TV on too loud after it got dark. But they also talked to me about things I didn't understand, like their houses getting broken into or seeing people fight in the street or people they knew who had died. Brittany said she saw somebody get shot in the alley behind her house. I'd only seen guns on TV, on the news, and on posters with big red X's across them. I asked her why, and she just shrugged and rubbed her two front fingers against her thumb. "That's how it goes," she said to me. I thought about that moment a lot; when I was cooking or in the middle of long division, it would just come to mind, looking out my window and seeing a stranger bulled over in a muddy alley. We were both eleven, but Brittany was older than me in a way that years couldn't account for.

Art

It was probably my mom who got me into growing. She kept orchids in the kitchen, tall with deep dark purple petals and white edges. She kept them away from the windows and stopped me from putting them in the sun and pouring my half-filled water glasses into the pots. "Everything comes up different, Art. This is what an orchid needs," she'd say, and touch one of the feathery little petals. She kept a garden behind our house, too. She tried to grow vegetables, but dogs and animals dug under the chain-link fence and tore up the vines. Planted gardenias one year, but they froze when winter came early.

She always came back to her orchids in the kitchen, training tiny flowers around chopsticks stuck in the soil. I liked watching her tie off the branches with twist ties. I liked helping her dig in the backyard. Even then, I liked the idea of helping things grow.

Growing was a decent alternative to kicking it on the corner. Before I found that Dank, I didn't know what I was going to do. All I knew was it had to be something that could get me off Sixty-seventh Avenue. That after-school-special shit didn't apply to me. Being an upstanding citizen in the village won't get you anywhere. A hustler or a fiend or a sucker, those were the options if you stayed local. If you wanted out, you needed money, and the way to get paid was to get with a crew. But I didn't want a street profile with the cops or the boys on the block. I hung out on the corner a little here and there, but I kept my head down. I played video games and stayed fucking inside.

The summer I was fifteen, I went out with my boy Tre over to Big Londell's. He's a block boy we'd known forever. He always had good weed, and Big Lon would smoke us out if we ran to the corner store for him. The man was huge on account of all the pork rinds and Twix bars he'd send us out for. One night, Big Lon sent Tre out for sodas and Swishers, and he started talking about the latest crop of herb he was bringing up. Said the plants were taller than him and the buds thick as a fist.

"Come on, son. Let me show you some real Dank shit," Big Lon said, and nodded me toward the back of the house. In a back bedroom with a wool blanket stapled across the window, a mess of furry branches and leaves sat under a buzzing light chained from the ceiling. I hadn't seen anything like it—green shoots reached up to my shoulders through squares of white twine, supporting stalks that were starting to show little buds at the top. "That's what's up," I said. "How many you got?"

"About sixty."

"When they gonna be ready?"

Big Lon smirked. "Soon enough. These babies just started flowering."

All the plants had been trimmed into three fat branches. Looked like a bunch of bright green pitchforks stacked up on their sides. The whole garden was no bigger than a twin mattress, but it was thick with plants. They seemed like they were trying to push one another out of the way to get more of that orange light. "How come the light's at an angle?"

Big Lon pointed to some shorter plants in the corner, where the light dipped down. "Give those little shorties some extra light. They indicas, so they won't grow as tall as the rest."

"Why you got these ones bent?"

"They're the most mature. About done. I just want them to get another week in, fatten them up." Big Lon pointed to the chicken wire tacked against the wall. Some of the plant stems were pinned into upside-down L's. "If you make them grow sideways, you get more fat tops."

"How that work?" I leaned into the bushes. They smelled fresh and full of water. The buds were pale green and thick with little white hairs. I squeezed a little bud top and released. My fingertips were sticky and stinky with resin. Big Lon slapped my shoulder. "Don't touch, kid."

After a while, Big Lon started rolling his eyes and making this bored sigh whenever I asked him a question about the set-up. He stopped answering my questions and went to rolling a blunt. He fished behind his couch and tossed a folded soft-cover book at me, not a real book but a copy. It read "The Closet Cultivator's Guide" in Sharpie marker on the front page, and the other pages were soft and creased, soft from someone flipping through quickly again and again.

I hunkered down in the hallway and read that manual all the way through. I'd never read anything that quick. It was the first time I wanted to read a book like that. I did okay in school, but I never put much into it. The schools on my side of town were a joke. Shit was falling apart even when some kid wasn't trying to destroy it. My teachers were young and wore khakis and Birkenstocks, and they were always scared shitless. Gave us handouts, put on videos, and left as soon as they could get reassigned to schools in Berkeley or Piedmont.

When Big Lon gave me that book, it was the first thing I wanted to learn about. It all made sense, the chemistry and the mechanics, how the plants would respond to certain stimulants. That night I sat in Big Lon's hallway reading about nitrogen levels and signs of plant anemia. It gave me this weird kind of comfort. Plants could be strong, and cannabis seemed designed to withstand—it could survive just about anything that the elements could throw at it. Freeze it, starve it, flood it, cut it in half, and it would still keep on. I liked that idea. Cut a stalk, cut off a limb, practically butcher the thing, but give it a few days and a little water, and three new stems will appear in its place.

Joanne

I'd been smoking in high school, at first just because it was the thing to do, but then I figured it out by accident how helpful weed could be after I smoked a blunt and plowed through four chapters of calculus. I could never keep my head on whatever we were talking about in class; my mind would just drift around like a bird from tree to tree. We had an exam for calculus worth a big chunk of our grade, and everyone was blowing it off. My dad knew I was cutting class and had been on me about my grades, so I knew I had to at least try. It was the night before, and I didn't know where to start or how, so I just took out my textbook when Freddy and Brittany and I were finishing a joint at the park. Something clicked—sine, cosine, tangent suddenly stood up and arranged themselves in a way that made sense. Freddy laughed hella hard when we all got our tests back, said he was trying my method next time. After that, Mary Jane was my study buddy.

Most people don't believe me, but Mary Jane helped me see what my teachers rambled about in class, really see it beyond the chunks of words in my textbook. When I first started out at the nursing program at the college, I'd smoke with my textbook in front of me. The skinless red body on the page opened up, expanded, became a model that I could pick up, take apart. I could see blood cells oxygenating, the contracting and constricting of veins in the ankles, the elbows, the heart. I could see the tick of neural waves, little zaps and clicks working their way up and down the spinal column. Muscles turned into segments of ropes, and each rope was made of threads, and those threads were bundles of fibers that formed according to function—stocky-celled muscles that contracted and flexed, smooth cellless orbs that stretched and anchored muscle to bone. I watched cells split and replicate, the nucleus becoming nuclei, and in the midst of tearing apart, the DNA molecules swirled inside, hinging and unhinging like spokes in a clock. I could walk up that double helix and name each of the complementary bases that made it, like rungs on a ladder—adenine to thymine, guanine to cytosine, backward and forward, again and again and again, spiraling up over my head and far below my feet. Inside every cell was instructions for every protein the body would ever produce, everything the body would ever need to function, their order and purpose precise, elegant, perfect.

I knew this hippy kid Randy who could get me weed. He was at the lake just about every day, real easy to find. He'd taken care of me for a long time, that is until he knifed some guy in the city and got sent up to county. I was high and dry, and I didn't like it. I tracked down Brittany. She and I went to the same community college, but we didn't see much of each other since we were in different programs. She was in the industrial arts program, learning to weld patch holes onto old car doors. In her spare time at the shop, she made metal stick figures with flash-melted joints and limbs bent under blue flame, little copper dancers with arched backs and tilting heads.

Brittany's hookup was in her neighborhood off Twenty-ninth Avenue, a good twenty minutes from my dad's house near the lake. "Call my boy Art. He'll take good care of you," she said over fries in the cafeteria. At first, I didn't want to travel that far—east O is just a few miles from Lake Merritt, but it's a world away from the coffee shops and farmers' markets by the lake, a trek into old industrial graves, little neighborhoods nestled between shuttered warehouses and factories. It's a sea change in a fifteen-minute stretch.

So I called Art. He didn't pick up but called me back a few minutes later. He gave me directions, so I made my way through downtown's office buildings and across Chinatown. I crossed the bridge off East Twelfth Street that went over the freeway and into the industrial zone, and I passed the old shipping yards and the warehouses that my dad used to work at when he was my age. Just about all of the buildings were shuttered and closed. I turned onto East Eleventh and drove past a trucking bay and a bunch of trucks and tractors lined up, until I came to the corner with the upside-down stop sign. Art was sitting on a porch. He came down and stepped into my passenger side. It's stupid, but in my memory that moment slows down, him crossing the street to jump in my car. Cinnamon skin and a clean fade, thick shoulders, but lean in all the right places—I could tell by how he walked, the way his white tee flagged at his sides. He smiled wide the first time he looked at me, this big dopey smile that was all teeth and gums. And I forgave him for that stupid gangster strut he did when he crossed the street to meet me. I smiled back before I could stop myself.

Art hopped in and out of my car those first few times, but soon we started driving around the block and sharing a joint, talking while blue smoke drifted out of the sunroof. He called me College Girl. He would pick up my textbooks off the passenger seat and flip through them, pointing and twisting his face at a picture of a diseased limb or a butterflied section of liver. He kept asking me to have a drink with him, and I always told him, "I bet you give all the ladies that line." He always shook his head and said, "Naw, girl, just you." I didn't want him thinking he could smoke me out and get in my pants. It was easier for me to have him in my car, where we could roll around the neighborhood talking, and I could drop him off at any corner I felt like.

The more we talked, the more he didn't seem like the hustlers on the corner. We talked about the factories that dotted his neighborhood, and the bay rappers who were just starting to get airplay on MTV. One afternoon I told him all about the axial skeleton because I had a test on it the next day, and he listened and asked me questions. He sang, "The frontal bone's connected to the...what did you call it? The accidental bone?"

I laughed. "Occidental," I said, tapping the back of his head where the soft ridge of the plate lay beneath his skin.

He wasn't fazed. "I like how I said it better."

A few weeks after I first started going to Tortilla Flat, and we'd been hanging out long enough that we had a regular route that we drove while we smoked, I turned to him one day and asked, "Aren't you gonna invite me in some time?"

He had a two-story sandwiched between another old house and a shabby little warehouse. The house looked like it hadn't seen a fresh coat of paint in a hundred years. It used to be blue, but it had chipped and faded to a grayish color that looked like a month-old bruise. It was simple inside—a few couches against the wall, DVDs and video games stacked in precarious columns next to the TV, a glass bong on the coffee table—and it was pretty clean, considering. Every time I came over, there was a dusting of weed bits across the coffee table, and the ashtray was piled high with shreds of tobacco that had been gutted from cigars.

We didn't grow up too far from each other, it turns out. It's not much of a surprise. The town can be pretty small. He was from the villages and knew some of my cousins who lived there. One day, we were on his couch in the front room laughing about something, I don't even remember what—some joke from Dave Chappelle, I think. We were sitting next to each other, close enough that our knees kept brushing whenever one of us moved. We were buzzed, and I was giggling, and he moved his arm over my head until he had my neck cradled in his elbow. He brought me to him and kissed me soft. I held my drink in the air like I was waiting for someone to take it so I could reach my arms around him.

Before long, I was hanging out there with Art almost every day, sipping the afternoons from a heavy whiskey glass. It was lovely. I'd run with him to drop bags off sometimes. Other times I would study in the living room while he worked in the garage. Sometimes he'd come out of the garage or just turn to me from the TV, take my book from my lap then crawl into it, press his forehead against my sternum. "I hear you thumping in there," he'd say, and work his way to my neck. I became a kind of background fixture, reading in the corner while he was talking to his people or working in the garage. My notebooks were always on the coffee table as improvised coasters. At some point, I started keeping my clothes there, started buying milk and cereal and eggs for the house. I didn't mind the drive from Twenty-ninth. There wasn't much traffic to the college in the morning.

My dad noticed I was gone. It was impossible not to, I guess. I tried to come home every day or two, tidy up a bit and cook a meal before I ran out the door back to Art's place. But I couldn't wiggle my way around my bed not being slept in. I usually said I was staying at Brittany's place, and even though he never called me on it, I knew he didn't buy it. If he knew where I was going and what I was going to, he wouldn't have been happy. "Tortilla Flat is a dump. Stay out of there," he said when I mentioned I'd come from across International Boulevard. He would find something to complain about—the bathroom stank or he hadn't eaten well in weeks. I was always trying to get out the door, so I would make him a pastrami sandwich and some eggs, and say I'd be back sometime tomorrow. Sometimes the easiest thing to do with the man was to say as little as possible. Once he went to work, I took a shower and packed some fresh clothes. I left a note for Leslie to tell her to make some pasta for dinner that night—she was seventeen, and I figured it was her turn to take care of the house for a change—and I left for Twenty-ninth.

It was a while, a few months, before Art showed me the grow room. That's how I knew we were getting serious, that we were doing more than passing the time with each other. He was already up when I rolled out of bed, and I could hear him and Londell talking downstairs. I waited for one voice to fall away and for the slam of the front gate—I always did—and for Art to come get back under the covers with me. But instead he called me downstairs. I stepped into the fuzzy slippers that I had brought over and trampled down the hardwood stairs. I found him in the kitchen, eating the leftover Chinese takeout from the night before. He kissed me and tasted like ginger, and I licked the oil off my lips.

The padlocks on the garage doors, always bolted, were unlocked. He had never said anything to me about it, and I never asked—I had been waiting for him to invite me in. "Lemme show you something," he said, and kissed me again.

I put my hand against the door, and the wood felt warm under my palm. Art smiled and jiggled the lock. When he opened the door, a gasp of hot air pushed at our faces. I stepped in—it was like a clean room at a hospital, everything lined with plastic or shiny metal. The whole room was bathed in Tang-colored light, no shadows anywhere. All kinds of plants were perched under four big lights. I felt my eyes widen and retract from the light at once—it almost made my eyes hurt. They were all uniform in length, but some had yellow splotches around their edges, and some had almost no leaves at all, just furry little buds forming up and down the stalks. I had never seen so many. In the corner was a closed door with white light radiating from beneath the doorjamb. I pointed to it. "What's in there?"

"That's what I'm fittin' to show you," he said, his mouth stuck in a smile. "She's my other baby." Art went over, played with the combination lock, and opened the second door. It was a closet lined completely in that shiny metal, like tin foil, but heavier. Three plants as big as saplings stood in wood planter boxes, which looked like wine barrels cut in half. The tops were tall as me and thick like big shrubs. A fan blew air upward from the floor, and a white light buzzed about two feet from the top leaves. "When are you going to get them flowering?"

Art plucked at one of the branches sticking out toward us. "These are mother plants. We don't let them bud. We keep them in the vegetative phase so they get nice and big, and we cut off the little stems. That's how we make clones." He turned a branch upward, displaying a stem with two sprigs with baby leaves unfurling from them. "We cut right here," he said, pointing just below where the branch had sprouted its leaves. Out in the garage in the corner was a little radio. Jazz played just loud enough to be heard over the fans.

"You always play music for them?"

He scratched his head. "Music helps them develop quick. I read this thing that said plants can grow up to three times faster in environments where music is playing."

"Any kind of music?"

"Jazz and classical had the best results. Rock and talk radio didn't produce the same effect."

I laughed and told him he was real smart. He said not to forget it and licked his lips. I got that blooming feeling in the small of my back, and it edged all through me, radiating out from the curve of my spine through to my fingernails and the tips of my feet. I kissed Art and smelled sweet fresh dirt waiting for seeds.

Art

I came up all right helping out Big Lon's people. I started out like a bunch of cats from the block, just getting rid of sacks for Big Lon here and there for the extra cash. I was always trying to fuck around with Big Lon's garden though. I had read that manual through and through, and I thought I knew everything about it back then. I bet I bugged the shit out of him with all of my suggestions. It was just that I saw so many ways he could make his garden produce more than he was getting. He probably let me make my initial adjustments just to shut me up. He was almost as surprised as I was when his yield doubled. I still got rid of bags for him, but I was the only one who could make adjustments to his operation from then on. Soon, I was doing the same for some of his boys' gardens. They all started calling me Green Thumb when I was doing work, Green Lung when we were smoking.

Big Lon called me Professor, liked to joke to his homies about my de facto degree in botany whenever he'd send me over. I hooked up sacks to this anthropology student at the Berkeley campus, and he let me use his student ID to get into the stacks. I wished that I could have just done that instead of going to school. If I could have floated around in a big library and read and studied whatever I wanted to, well, I probably would have done more than just show up and pass through. It surprised me that I even graduated. In the stacks, I felt at home. No one bothered me in there or gave me shit about having my nose in a book. I could just find a couch and read and read. The librarian up there got to know me. She thought I was a graduate student, said that no one spends that much time in the library unless they have to.

At first, I just read the gardening books they kept in the general-purpose library, but the botanical chemistry books were a lot more useful to my work. Once I understood the peptide structures and the metabolic processes of the plant, and how they could be manipulated, it was cake. It was simple chemistry, most of it: sodium, potassium, carbon, hydrogen, nitrogen. The building blocks of everything. I spent most of my time in the sciences wing. I read up on hydroponics and plant genetics, how to make strains heartier, how to make them more adaptable, which amino acid and protein combinations would improve strength, quality, and quantity. I took everything in and brought it back to Big Lon's garden. Practical applications. Straight muthafuckin' academics.

What I didn't know I picked up from this hydroponics shop down in Hayward off Mission. I was in there so much the boss gave me a job. My first day in the shop, I set up this display of thousand-watt lights and reflective aluminum sheets with a pot of yellow geraniums underneath, and this billboard that read "New Techniques for a New Millennium."

I was doing all right for myself. Generally satisfied. With most people I helped out, it was usually a matter of pH balance, the timing of when plants needed more carbohydrates or less exposure to the lights. At first it was no big thing. People had a few dozen plants in an extra bedroom or a basement, and I'd just make the adjustments or test the soil, and I'd be out. I guess Big Lon had spread the word, because he started sending me out to bigger operations. The first big op was this warehouse off Fifth Street, near the ports. We drove around the building, parked, and went to a boarded-up door. A guy even bigger than Big Lon opened the door, the handle of his glock sticking out of his waistband. If the people at the other sites I had done work at were strapped, they didn't make a point of letting me know like this guy. I put my game face on and stepped inside. The garden was huge, over three hundred plants at different levels of growth. A lot of money growing, and a lot of money invested. This was not small time. I kept reminding myself to just look at the plants, not at faces, just get the shit over with. It didn't get easier ignoring those fools with guns, no matter how many times I did it. I was always paranoid that some hothead kid would be playing with his pistol and pop one off into my fucking head by accident. I always did the job as quick as I could and got the hell out.

I moved into this rickety old house over in Tortilla Flat off East Eleventh, a blue two-story that had seen better days, but she was just right. Cheap, secluded, and the garage windows were already painted over. I started my own garden, worked out the kinks of mass production, finding the right combination of peptides and amino acids in the nutrient mix. I kept the best nutrient combinations to myself. All the time that I was working for Big Lon and his people, I wondered how I wanted this career path to play out. I was making decent money setting up gardens, and Big Lon made sure to take good care of me. I was making him and his people fat stacks, I knew that.

Some days I could never see getting out of the town. I liked having my finger on the pulse, keeping up on all the major growers, being a part of town business. I liked doing the club hustle with Big Lon and the boys, being in the thick of all these kids and people trying to be kids on the dance floor. Nothing like knowing all the security guards and the bartenders and the back entrances. The good life you only see on TV. It was the sweet hustle, drinking with breezies and slipping sacks in their purses. A world away from handing shit off on the corner.

But on other days, I wanted to move to the forest up north and have a garden up in the hills, all my weed au naturel. Soil and sun and not a damn thing else. On some days that sounded real good, especially the days when I was setting up grow rooms for people who had a grow room on one side of the building and a cook house on the other. I could see myself up in the woods living in a log cabin, just me and my babies. It would be like camping every day.

Sometimes Jo and I talked about it, how selling sacks was always going to be small time, unless you were on the supply side of things. I couldn't get enough of that girl. Smart as hell, sweet too. She wasn't some hood rat trying to get smoked out for free. I could have been happy every day of my life if I could just play with her hair all I wanted. She had a mess of black curls, tight corkscrews that were made to fit around my fingers. I'd spring a curl between my fingers, and we'd talk about the garden, the future. She would turn around, palm my scalp like she was holding my head in place, and tell me not to worry. "You can get your own ends with your own garden. You'll figure out a way." I wanted to believe her. I wanted to believe that there was a way to set myself up, make something out of myself. Working for Big Lon, my expertise was always to someone else's advantage, someone else's profit.

One day I was helping this crew set up an op in an old port warehouse off High Street. Big Lon sent me over to set up their nutrient regulation system. I had an aversion to hydroponics, though I could admit it was the best mode of rapid production. It felt like Frankenstein shit: plants that didn't need soil, just a constant stream of water, a timed drip of nutrients, and a rope to wrap their roots around. The process created plants that were overstimulated, overfed, overgrown, and stunted at the same time. But I looked at their size and did the calculations in my head, and they were going to be producing almost two pounds per cycle, and they'd have a cycle up for harvest once a month.

I found one of the guys running the show, the scrawniest one that seemed the most enthusiastic. The chatty ones always let the important stuff slip out. "So how you going to move all that? Are you sending some out into the world?" I figured they must have been shipping it east. A pound of Cali Green was worth three times as much if you could get rid of it on the East Coast.

"This isn't for the street. We're straight vendors, bro," the kid said to me, and pulled a laminated card out from his back pocket. Next to a bad passport picture and his name and address were imprints by the state of California and the city of Oakland. "Patient Vendor" was stamped in red across medicinal marijuana ordinance numbers. "This is the shit that's poppin' now."

The medicinal clubs had been around for a few years, but I thought it was bullshit. It seemed like the only people who could get Prop 215 protection were hippies growing in Humboldt or rich cancer patients in Santa Barbara that were too good for chemo. But it was becoming the real thing. I had heard about it from Big Lon and from some of the smokers I knew from the hydro shop. We drove through downtown Oakland to Broadway, and between the old theaters and the coffee shops were storefronts with mirrored windows or a security guard posted outside. One night, Big Lon got us into a medical club on Mission. One of Big Lon's people was involved on the supply end of things for the club, and he arranged to let us in and check the spot out.

The cats running the joint had it set up like a real pharmacy. All their permits were framed on the walls. There were big jars that marked each strain, vials of hash oil, a refrigerator full of edibles, and security cameras in each corner of the ceiling. Call it business, call it my blossoming entrepreneurial sense, or just call it the American dream, whatever the fuck that is. I wanted on that club train. Being hood rich and stuck helping out the Sixty-seventh boys didn't satisfy, knowing there was a legit way to get paid. Suddenly I had a new vision as I tended to my own garden. I'd be sitting behind a desk in a brightly lit office, jars of weed in a glass case and my state license framed on the wall over my head.

There was this cat Khaled in the city that I used to kick it with, a hustler in the clubs and into other shit that I figured I didn't want to know about. Khaled had his own club above a bar in the Mission called the Hourglass, and he didn't mind me hustling my sacks here and there. I used to chill with him at night after we finished. This one night at his crib, he had eight-grand worth of thizz tabs in front of him when the city was dry as a bone. I shit you not, it was a sugar mountain of baby blue pills. And this cat was throwing his cell phone across the room, telling dealers to fuck off. That's some shit, to control the supply and tell the fiends to wait for the call. Khaled had it locked, sitting at this big desk with a stack of bills on one side and a box full of pills on the other. I'll be damned if I didn't like it. I wanted to be sitting on the best shit, whatever it was, and say yes and no to whomever the fuck was asking. That was king shit.

After I looked into it and found out about how to get the permits, I figured out how much I'd need to get my own club going—a storefront and a steady supply, plus security, and I was sure there would be some wheels to grease in whatever neighborhood I ended up having my shop. I needed some front money, and I couldn't go to Big Lon. He liked me just where I was, as a goddamn worker bee, and he didn't want me doing anything on my own. So I went to Khaled to see if he could help me drum up some cash.

"Capital investment," Khaled smirked when I laid out my plan.

He fronted me some E tabs to get rid of across the bridge. Nothing too big, but enough that I could get some return on it. Khaled was helping me get my money clean by writing me checks through the Hourglass. Every package was money toward the license and permits, toward new equipment and new strains. I got it all off my hands quicker than I thought. After a few months and a few packages, I was in it. I was getting decent weight off the home operation. I was making plans to file my paperwork as a vendor soon and anxious to start looking at retail spaces in Hayward. I could see myself in an office, suit and tie if I wanted. My club up and running, and I'd spend my days managing and my nights working in my gardens. I'd go home to Jo in her little white nursing uniform. We'd have a little place up in the hills where we could see the whole bay. She was always talking about wanting a dog, that she'd never had one, and I'd give her one, a big slobbery pit bull, whatever she wanted. I'd get her a grip of dogs, I'd get her jewelry, even though she swore up and down she didn't want any. I wanted to give her whatever she wanted, all the things she said she didn't need.

Joanne

Art always locked up tight behind him when he left the house. He kept all his keys on a big ring that could fit around my wrist, and he would go through all the locks, checking each one twice before moving on to the next. I always teased him about it and said it was his OCD coming out. He'd just say he was being thorough.

It was a Thursday, Thizz Night at the El Portal in Richmond. Art was out with some of his boys. I hated those nights out at the club—always a bunch of kids from Walnut Creek and Danville slumming it, going out and trying to act grown, drinking too fast and talking too much. I decided to stay home that night. I could hang at the house, do my work for class, watch TV, and wait for Art to get back from the rounds. He and his boys never came home until after two or three. I helped him pick out a jersey and a fitted cap to wear that night—all black and silver Raiders gear. We smoked a blunt before he and the boys went out. I listened to Art's keys working the dead bolts, and when the locks fell silent, I went and cracked a beer and spread out in the living room.

I fell asleep on the couch. I always pass out there, and Art would tease me about it when he would come home. He would find me stretched out with my books all open, the blunt burned out and my beer warm.

It's better that I was out there in the front. I'd taken off my shoes, but at least my shorts were still on.

It's crazy. I felt something in my sleep. It's hard to explain, how your body knows someone else is there, how it can sense these things even when your mind is asleep. Another peripheral nervous system that isn't tuned to the mind, but somewhere below the brain, I think. Some force that lives above your gut and between your lungs, traces up and down the spinal cord. I woke up already afraid. It had hold of my chest before I felt that grip on the top of my head.

Someone yanked my hair from behind and pulled me up. He shouted at me: "Who else is here? Where they at?"

I like to think I'm in control of myself. I always thought if I were put in this kind of situation, I wouldn't react. But damn it, I did. I hate that I screamed. I felt something hard and cold dig at my neck, and that scream just clawed its way out of me. I bet they thought I was easy after that.

I stumbled off the couch and swiveled from the fistful of hair he had me by. I couldn't see the man pushing me. He kept the gun between my shoulder blades and kept hold of my hair. His masked face was craned over my neck. He smelled like oil and sweat, like something fried. Nasty. He pushed me down the hall-way and into the corner of the garage by the open door. My back was to the wall. I still don't know how they got that door open, how they pried off all the locks without me waking up.

There were three others, all in black coats, two with pistols, and a fat one with a shotgun balanced across his shoulders. They wore sunglasses and stupid grins. The fat man was standing by the mother closet where the big plants were. He was looking at the white light emanating from the cracks of the door.

He pushed at the combination lock over the handle with the wooden butt of the shotgun. "Unlock it," he said as Fry Boy came in front of me.

It was an inch from the bridge of my nose—the business end of that gun. Even if I knew the combination, I couldn't have told them. Every part of me was fixed on that gun. Black metal blurred back, the connected arm and face fading behind the gap-ing hole. In the background were pages of an anatomy book flip-ping randomly: exit wounds, flesh splayed away from cadavers, brown blood curdling in the throat. The whole world swirled into a black point, a pinprick tear in the universe. It seemed to wink at me.

"I don't know how." The words sputtered out. I could only see that hole pressing at me. I didn't want a matching one in my skull.

I waited for them to say, "You lyin," but instead, one of them came up and started on the hinge with the butt of his pistol. It came off after a few good swings. The fat one stepped into the closet.

Fry Boy pulled the muzzle away a bit, enough for my focus to blur. "This is a surprise, baby doll." The fat one smelled the mother plants and stuck his ugly face into the branches huffing on that smell. They were as tall as the room and green like the Oakland hills after rain. The fat one started touching on the leaves. He turned and tried pulling the planter boxes out into the garage. He got winded and motioned one of the smaller guys over to help him. One of the boys got behind the biggest mother, the trainwreck plant, and they pushed its planter box across the garage, then moved the rest of the mothers into the middle of the garage. The boys bitched the whole time about how heavy the plants were.

The other two were looking around the room, touching the babies, sizing up the operation. The fat one stood in the doorway and turned to me in the corner.

"Don't sweat, sugar pie. This is a courtesy call." His voice was thick. "Tell your little boyfriend that he won't be doing shit on this side no more." With that, he nodded to the others and walked out of the garage. One of them came up beside me, took my arm, and stabbed the muzzle back up against my ribs.

They started with the mothers, tearing each out by its stalk base, throwing them down and chucking the planters across the garage. One of them took out a knife and drew a slash across the fertilizer bags in the back. It spilled out in a gush, all that soft dirt. They knocked bottles and cleansers off the shelf and began punting them against the far wall, next to where I stood pinned. Sometimes a bottle would explode, and the cleansers and thick plant food would spray across my feet and legs. I heard heavy footsteps above the garage. It had to be the fat one climbing the stairs.

I could taste the bleach as they poured a big bottle over the mothers and into each of the plants, then tossed the green plastic pots against the brick wall. They did this for a while, until the one throwing the pots seemed to get tired. He rubbed his shoulders from the work. They finally just doused the plants in wide sloshes over the garden, pushing a pot over here and there. I jumped every time a pot smacked to the floor. Within a minute or two, the leaves began to pale. They curled into themselves, like they'd been blanched in boiling water. They died that quick.

It all went down in six minutes. My eyes wandered from the gun to the wall clock, that second hand ticking as slow as an IV drip. What brought me out of it was the sparks from the lights breaking. One of them went into the mother closet and took the butt of his gun to the electric lights lining the walls. The other one reached up to the ceiling and tore down the four light tracts. They crunched the lightbulbs under their boots. The yellow lights crackled and spat sparks.

It went black in the garage, save for the weak light cast

underneath the hallway door. The two boys knocked the soggy bits of dirt off their boots by kicking the wall close to me. I didn't hear what they were saying as they walked out of the garage.

The one next to me turned in front to face me and tugged at my hair so that I stood up on the balls of my feet. He rested the barrel against my cheek. Time expanded, contracted, then collapsed onto itself in the dark pit of that muzzle.

"It's been fun, sugar pie," Fry Boy said, his voice like sandpaper. He tilted my head and kissed me hard on the lips. I felt his teeth behind his lips and through the knit mask, the hard grating of his mouth against mine. My lips tightened into a seal, my teeth made ready to bite, and then I felt the cool finish of the muzzle pressed against my cheek. I shrank into nothing, trying not to feel anything, hoping that this wasn't going to be the last thing I felt before I died. I waited for the click, the final tug that would trail through my skull. But he shoved me down instead, and I heard the door slam behind him.

One of the lights fizzled on and off. I was light-headed. That bleach was clawing at my nose and my throat. I could barely breathe. My ass hurt where he pushed me down. The ground was wet with bleach and damp dirt, spiked with broken glass. I wanted to stand up but couldn't. My body didn't want to come back to me. My limbs refused to work, paralyzed by the cold in the room, still held hostage by that gun, the ghost of its shape hovering in front of me. All the heat in the room came from the lights, and with them busted, the room went cold quick. I heard footsteps upstairs, and I heard laughing. I wondered where Art was, and then I wondered if they were done with me, if they weren't going to come back. My hand searched and found a bottle that had a long sharp edge. I grabbed it by the neck—a bit of glass dug into my palm—and pushed myself back into the corner where they put me, not sure what I would do if they came back. Everything was wet and cold and covered with dirt. I pushed my hair out of my face and found a leaf, still green, caught in my curls.

I thought of the first planting that Art brought me in on a few months back, when that trainwreck mother was no taller than my kneecaps. When that mother had just pushed out its first full branches, we huddled in that closet, me inside that egg-white room with no shadows, Art over me in the door frame. He packed the baby sprouts into spongy sections of silt as quickly as I cut them off the mother's branches. He smiled as he set the little clones into a baking tray with a bit of water at the bottom. "Didn't I tell you money grows on trees, Jo Jo?"

I thought about Art, and I thought about my dad, how he would shit a brick if he saw me like this, huddled in a garage full of dead weed plants. My chest was suddenly seizing, my lungs contracting. I had only known this kind of fear through empathy, listening to shouts and shots off in the distance. A spasm went through me, the sensation of blood flow flooding through veins, forcing constriction, the muscle catching hold of a nerve and jangling it back and forth, the whole homeostatic system trying to reorder itself. I wanted out of that garage. I wanted to stop shaking. I wanted to go home.

Art

The boys dropped me off around three. We'd had a good night, had fun at the club, got rid of everything we came with. I was feeling generous, bought Rémy Martins all around. I was wishing

Jo was with me—I expected her to be in bed or on the couch, passed out. She'd wake up and follow me upstairs, her hand in mine when we'd walk to my room in the dark.

I was walking up the path to the house. I was whistling, until I got to the porch. The screen was unlocked, and the front door was open. Jo knew to never leave the front door open, even when I was home. I didn't search for my keys, just pushed my way in.

At first, the only thing that was wrong was the front door being open. For a minute I thought maybe I was just paranoid, that the street was starting to get to me. But the love seat was moved, wedged in the hallway against the garage door. I yelled out Jo's name, but she didn't answer. I moved the love seat out of the way and pulled the door open. I don't know what I was expecting, but I already knew it was bad. I could feel it like a rock rolling around in the pit of my stomach. The lights were bashed, and I smelled something awful. It was a goddamn terrible mess, and I didn't need the lights to see that everything was fucked. The mound of dirt on the floor looked like a body. It took a second for my eyes to adjust enough. The mound on the floor was my crop. One hundred and thirty-seven plants. Four months of work turned to a mess of dirt and broken green pots across the floor. The lights were out. Nothing worth trying to salvage left.

I didn't see Jo until I heard something shift behind me. She was tucked in the corner. Light from the hall lit up on her shins. Every part of her was in the dark, except those long shins, almost glowing. I reached down to get her, and she jabbed at me with a broken bottle, held up one arm to her face and whacked at the air with the other. I caught her arm and pulled her up. She was so heavy. "Baby, it's me. It's me," I kept saying. Blood had dried on her arms, patches of it still wet.

I picked her up and took her out of there, then laid her down on the couch. Her shirt was damp, and her face was all puffy. She didn't say anything, just kind of stared at me. I wiped the dirt off her knees and wrapped an afghan we had in the living room around her shoulders. I said her name again and again. It felt like someone was strangling me from inside my chest. She tucked her chin against her and wouldn't say anything, just worked her hand around the neck of that broken bottle.

I left her there and went upstairs. For the first time in my life I wanted a piece, some big bore-heavy caliber "what, you wanna fuck with this?" piece. I grabbed the metal bat I kept beside the front door and gripped the handle tight.

They took everything, and what they didn't take, they fucked up just for the hell of it. There was nothing left of the plants when I went back into the garage with a flashlight. They did a good job of making sure I couldn't do anything for a while. I pieced through the broken pots and wondered if that was the whole point, to slow me down and remind me of the pecking order. I never got anyone's permission to be doing things in this neighborhood. I was running shit for Khaled on what was definitely someone else's turf. My head spun with all the possibilities of who it could be. I had forgotten how small the town could be.

That's when I ran upstairs to the hallway closet. I kept the pills from Khaled in a zipped-up duffel bag underneath a boxful of old clothes. I made myself look, hoping they were just cats that were mobbing stupid and happened to rush the right place. I dug through the closet. Everything was out of place, like they had done a clean sweep of each shelf until they found what they were looking for. They had even pulled up a few of the floor-boards in the closet to make sure I hadn't hidden anything else.

Everything was gone. All of Khaled's stash, everything I stockpiled. I almost fell against the wall behind me. Fucked didn't even begin to describe the situation.

I went back downstairs and tried to calm down. I locked the screen door and the front door. I was pacing. I couldn't stop moving. I didn't know what I would feel if I stopped. Everything told me to keep moving, stay mad. I paced across the living room. I wanted to punch a wall. I wanted to plant that bat into just the right skull. I wanted to go up into the village and talk to Big Lon. I wanted names. I wanted to unmake this whole night.

I was getting too agitated walking in circles, so I knelt in front of her on the couch. She hadn't moved since I put her on the couch.

"Did they touch you? Did they put a hand on—tell me what they looked like. Come on, Jo baby, tell me something." She met my eyes, but every time she opened her mouth, it was like the words were stuck in her. I grabbed her hands and felt dry blood crackle against my palms. She finally dropped the bottle in her lap. I squeezed her hands despite myself, and she sucked in air and let out a sound that was high and hot, with all different kinds of pain wrapped up into it. I let go, and her hands snapped back against her chest.

"Baby, talk to me. Tell me who it was. Tell me something. I'm gonna do something about this, so tell me. Tell me something." I could feel my voice rising but couldn't do anything about it though. Something in me was boiling over. Her hands were bloody. I should have been thinking about wrapping her up, pulling the glass out of her palms, but instead I wanted to match her blood with the ones that made her bleed. I was shaking her, my grip tight around her shoulders. I couldn't help it. Her silence was killing me more than the thought that those skeezy block boys had been in my house, taking what's mine. I must have been hurting her, but I couldn't tell, and at that moment, I didn't really care. "Fucking talk to me!"

"I can't!" she finally choked the words out. She was pulling away from me. "I don't..." Her face twisted up.

"Yes, you can, Jo baby. You got to. You have to." I pulled her close to me and held her there in a way I never had before. "Tell me, just tell me. Don't tell me you don't know anything." She struggled, and I kept her until she sprang out of my hold and threw her arms around my neck. She gripped on to me strong, and I didn't know if she was trying to hold me or hold me back. "You can't be like them," she said to me, gripped so tight around me I thought I'd choke. She cried and balled her fists against my ears. I gritted my teeth and breathed in, her hair brushing my face. Almost smelled sweet. Then I pushed her away.

She fell back on the couch and looked at me. She reached up. I thought she was going to hit me, but she put her hand just under my ear. She just held that part of my neck and looked at me.

I said the only thing I could. "I want them dead."

She nodded, and her face filled up like she was going to sob. "I know you do."

We stayed like that a while, just reading each other's eyes. Her eyes were like fog. I took her hand and looked at it. When I leaned down to kiss her fingertips, I saw the sliver of glass in her palm.

"Let me get this out."

Her palm curled up on itself, but she let it stay in mine.

I found some gauze and cleaned her up, picked the sliver out and wiped the blood off her arm. I made us each a brandy, threw the ice cubes in after I'd already poured the liquor. After she finished her drink in a long draw, she winced. "I'm a go back to my house a while," she said after a second. I didn't say anything. She was glazed, told me she wanted to go home, but she couldn't drive. I said I'd take her back, but we didn't move until the night was turning into morning. The last thing she told me was that she had class, that she was supposed to know all this stuff about the brain and neural impulses. She looked at me and said she had forgotten everything she learned the night before.

CHINTA'S
FABULOUS
TRAVELING SALON

"MARISSA!" CHINTA PULLS the phone cord as far as it will stretch around her desk, her palm pressed over the receiver. Marissa is behind the displays of beauty products, squawking like a parrot with Solange, who paints a pasty white coloring onto a tin-foiled section of a customer's hair. *Catty bitches,* Chinta thinks, adjusting the phone on her shoulder. She calls Marissa again, trying to be loud and at the same time polite. Marissa takes her time in turning to meet Chinta's eyes, and she stalks to the counter past the shelves of brightly colored bottles and jars, her heels clicking loud in the now-quiet salon.

"I got your 3:30 appointment on the phone. Says she's gonna be late," Chinta says, walking back around the corner to her desk directly in front of the entrance.

"Is it the style or the cut?" Marissa drums her nails against the desktop. Her eyelashes are too long to look anything but synthetic, and they *whisk-whisk-whisk* together as she speaks. Chinta imagines the lashes snapping shut like a Venus flytrap as she looks at the appointment book.

"Sonia. Color and style."

Marissa pushes past Chinta, who stretches the phone around her body. "Who else I got today?" she says, running a tangerine acrylic nail across the calendar, and sighs at how hard it is to have so many appointments. She steps out from the desk and pushes a yellow and purple lock of her weave over her shoulder. "Well, I'm booked up. You want to take it?" Marissa says, her eyes turning from Chinta to her nails. She works a bit of grit out from under her pinkie.

Chinta squirms, checking her watch against the time that she told her sister Christy she would be at the house. Cleaning houses was one of her many gigs spread across the week—day shifts at Tammy's, event service at the Indian restaurant, and an afternoon or two preparing unsold homes for Christy to show. It's 12:45, and she's supposed to be at the house at 1:30—Sonia won't arrive until 4 p.m. There's no way. Her eyes narrow at the appointment book, and she works the phone cord hard between her fingers. "I would, but I can't today. I'm off at one, and I got to be somewhere."

Marissa does that half smile—all shiny lipstick and no teeth—as if Chinta has just ruined her day. "What, you can't help me out?" She snaps her gum between her teeth.

Chinta brings the phone back up to her ear but keeps her hand pressed hard against the receiver. She wants to take the job, and Marissa knows it. Sonia wants a wash, cut, color, the whole works, and always gives the stylist a twenty on the way out the door. Eighty dollars in the register and half of it hers. A steady customer who might ask for her by name. *Any other day,* she thinks, *any other day and I could grab this job, show these bitches that if I could rent a chair, I'd be sitting pretty as them.* "I wish I could."

Marissa shrugs, bats her fake eyelashes. "I guess you don't need money or something," Marissa says, her hands on her hips.

"Well, tell Sonia to reschedule. She'll be happier with me doing it anyhow."

Chinta watches her swagger back toward the chairs. Marissa leans over Solange's shoulder and whispers, and they both giggle. Chinta removes her palm from the receiver and talks to the voice on the line. "I'm sorry, but Marissa can't make herself available this afternoon. May I reschedule you?"

Of course, the day she has to leave is the day Marissa says, "Take the big job." Marissa wouldn't really want to let Chinta work on one of her regulars. All the stylists at Tammy's never pass up the best jobs, just throw Chinta the scraps—the simple work they don't bother with when they can make some real money on a style or a weave or a treatment. They toss her the twelve-dollar trims, while they joke and gossip with the real clients, the ones they know will come back.

She watches the inching hands of the clock above the door, her right foot tapping anxiously against the leg of her stool. The hand-painted *Tammy's Cuts and Accents Beauty Salon* scrawled across the window blocks the sun trying to come through. She looks at Sonia's name in the book but reminds herself to be patient. She'll have plenty of hair to cut later tonight, if she can get through this house in time. As soon as the dial hand hits one, she grabs her purse from the drawer and slings it over her shoulder as she strides out from the desk. She calls out to the girls in the back, then waves to them from the open doorway. As soon as the glass doors stammer shut behind her, her smile drops and she imagines Solange's four-inch shears jammed in Marissa's ear. An inch for each month she's pretended not to hear them talk shit at the washing stations, ever since she had to call Tammy herself about Marissa and Solange cutting her out of the tips.

Her phone beeps when she gets to the car at the far end of the mall parking lot. Christy has been calling for the last half hour, trying to give Chinta the directions to the house. The stale heat in the car is thick against Chinta's skin, with patches of sweat forming at her brow and temples. She dials, rolls her neck, and waits for Christy to pick up.

"Where you been? Your mailbox is full," Christy huffed, her breath muffling against Chinta's ear.

"I was working. I left Tammy's just now." Chinta starts the engine, the alternator clicking in tired whirs before catching. She glares at the hood of her car. *Don't you go on me, too.*

"I've got that address for you. And finish it today. I want to be able to show it first thing in the morning." Christy sounds pissy. She prefers that Chinta take care of the houses early in the morning, get them cleaned and polished from top to bottom. Then in the afternoon, Christy can walk potential buyers through, pointing to spotless windows and dustless ceiling fans, their footprints disturbing Chinta's perfectly parallel vacuum tracks in the carpet.

"What? I'm in my car. I'm headed to the Fifties. Damn." Chinta let out a grumbling sigh so her sister knew that she didn't have the monopoly on shitty days.

"You're late, and that makes me late. You got a pen?" Christy reads her the address twice, and Chinta writes the house number on the back of her hand. Her sister's mantra when Chinta began cleaning the houses was that a sparkling house sells quickly. Not just clean, but *sparkling*. "A house is a house, no matter how clean it is," Chinta always snapped back when Christy dropped that nugget as they toured a new property, but Chinta could admit that presentation was half the battle.

Gripping the wheel, she lingers at the intersection when the light changes to green to study the chip on the design of her ring fingernail—one of the French tips is cracking, on the cusp of a full break. Chinta has small hands, small fingers. Rare miniatures, she and Gina and Leti always joked, especially when they were in high school, and Chinta wore a nail set of half-inch-long cat claws, always bright red or hot pink. She thought the nails made her hands look more graceful, more womanly, but instead, they accentuated just how childlike her hands were. Even now her fingers look stubby, and she wonders if everything about her tiny frame looks shrunken, smaller than it should be. Her instructor at the cosmetology school told her she had hands like a toddler, said it was a miracle she could hold her scissors and comb at the same time.

It's not far from Fruitvale to the house on Fifty-third Street—about fifteen minutes from Tammy's. The neighborhood is a low-lying block just below the slopes of the hills, each house surrounded by waist-high chain-link. Not a tree in sight. The house is a simple two-story, its front and backyard in bad need of some grass seed. It has a shady little porch in the front of the house, like nearly every house on this block. Its Frappuccino-brown coat of paint is so fresh that Chinta can smell it from the street. First things first. She walks to the Realtor's sign stuck in the corner of the lawn, unhinges the "For Sale" board, and slides the board with Christy's name and number and pixelated face off the white post. Into the backseat the sign goes; she will put it back later tonight, once she's cleaned the house and done her real work for the day.

Yesterday, after Christy told her about this house and that she'd have to take care of it in the afternoon, she put the word out to her compadres and the handful of people who have become her regulars: she'll be in the lower Fifties today doing a house, and if they need a cut, she'll be free in the afternoon. Chinta's Fabulous Traveling Salon is open at the brown house on Fifty-third Street, this afternoon only.

Two stories, three bedrooms, and two bathrooms—five hours or so, Chinta thinks as she wanders up the concrete walk to the front stoop. The lock gives, and she steps into the front room, surveying her job for the day. The walls are mayonnaise white, a brand-new coat that the sellers slapped on before they moved out. The ceilings are pimpled like a teenager's cheeks. Big sliding windows fill the room with sun. It's sweltering inside, and she struggles to pry the windows open so a breeze can push its way inside.

She tours the house, planning. Her rubber sandals slap against the stairs. If she hustles through the first level—sweeping, dusting, polishing every inch of wall and floor—she should finish without a hitch. The second floor will take time because of the carpeting, but she figures if she works fast, she'll be done by six, maybe even a bit earlier. Luckily, she doesn't have to address the kitchen. It's just been renovated with wooden cabinets, porcelain sinks, and a kitchen island made entirely of blue and green tiles. All that needs to be done is to get rid of the plastic sheeting the builders covered the floors with. She smiles. She'll leave it and set up her station here, where the plastic is still down. Then she can just ball up the hair in the plastic sheeting, rather than having to sweep it up at the end of the day. She kicks at a corner of the plastic, taped across the tiled kitchen floor. At the end of the day, she'll give the kitchen a good once-over to get any paint chips or dust that may have settled on the counters.

She heads to the car, pops the trunk. Chinta moves a month's worth of sweatshirts and random pieces of clothing, a grocery bag of shoes for her mom to give to the church thrift shop, and a half-empty case of bottled water before she unearths her cleaning supplies from the bottom of the trunk: two milk crates full of aerosol sprays and powder cleaners, spot and stain removers, sponges and dust rags and clean wipe cloths, brooms and mops, and the bucket that swings obnoxiously by its rickety handle. She lugs the crates out and is already sweating when she gets up to the house, a damp patch forming at the base of her neck and at her temples. Back at the car, she grabs her stash and her stereo, locks up and heads into the house.

Sitting on the back stoop with tufts of scrub grass pushing up around the concrete porch, she smokes a joint and is glad she's not at Tammy's right now. She's glad that she's not a jockey at the register. *Fuck them. I'm about to have my own chair in a few hours.* She smokes and studies the telephone wires intersecting over the houses, how they form black hatch marks against the blue sky.

She's excited. At least a few of the homies will roll through for a trim or a touch-up, and her homegirl Leti says she told one of her coworkers from the nail salon about her, and she might come, too.

It could be a good day for cutting, if she can get this house together quick enough. Plus, it will be a nice reunion. It's harder and harder to make time to see anyone these days. In the last year or so, some of her friends finished college, some had babies, some got married. Of course everyone has to work, nine to five and otherwise. She brushes the ash from her joint into the dirt and heads into the house, hoping the breeze picks up.

First, she turns on the radio to the hip-hop station and turns it up loud. She wraps her red-tinted curls into a knot at the crown of her head, then snaps on her plastic yellow gloves. Starting on the first floor, she scours the walls, sweeps the dust and cobwebs from the ceiling corners, scrubs the baseboards, and polishes the wooden paneling of the windowpanes and door frames.

Downstairs has hardwood floors, the red varnish worn to tan around the front door and the other entryways. Chinta considers the patches, how they must have developed from years of shoes shuffling over them. One family, probably more than one—many families call the same house "home" in some part of their history, their memory. Sometimes she thinks about that, how the houses she cleans are in photo albums, in snapshots with people smiling in bedrooms, around dining tables, in the backyard flourishing with green grass. Someone far away or maybe very close by thinks of this house, and maybe cries or feels their chest cave in just a little because now they can only drive past on the way to something more important, some newer house, some better life.

She works in time with the song playing on the radio—polishing in timed swirls, pushing the broom to the pattern of eight-count beats. By the time she's finished the downstairs front rooms, the small of her back nags at her with a dull ache, and her knees are sore from crouching. She feels damp as she climbs the stairs with her bottles and sponges, a film of sweat covering her face and arms and thighs. The air in the house is hot, but at least it's moving.

Hopping from bedroom to bedroom, she changes her approach—rather than knocking out one room at a time, she goes task by task. She scrubs all the walls, washes the inside and outside of all the windows, and then vacuums all of the carpeting.

The orange extension cord snakes behind her, leaving a slither across the perfect vertical tracks in the cream carpet. Between these tasks, her phone rings.

"Where you at today?" David says. Chinta can hear the clicking sounds of office work in the background. "You doing the thing?"

"You know it." Chinta turns off the vacuum and lets it slide out away from her before pulling it back into place. "I'm at the corner of Fifty-third Street off International. Come through around six."

"That don't work for me, girl," he says.

"I guess you outta luck," she retorts. "And some bootsy barber can mess you up again."

David does that nasally chuckle—quiet in the office. "Fine. I'll gun it back to the town when I get out. You better touch my fade up right."

She smiles. "Come through and I got you," she says, leaning away from the vacuum like a tuxedoed dancer kicking out from her cane. "I'm at the end of the block. You'll see my car in the driveway. And bring swishers."

Gina calls, too, and so does Leti, who wants to correct some blond highlights and maybe get some fresh ones. Every time she gets a call, Chinta feels excitement bloom in her stomach, and not just at the thought of an extra layer of bills in her wallet. She's happy to hurry through the house. She can't wait to get out her clippers, tug a section of hair straight, and feel the damp sprigs fall down at her feet.

It's almost six, and the sun is dipping into the power lines, its smoky red edge almost touching the roofs of the neighborhood. The last room to clean is the master bathroom, and in between scrubbing the tub and wiping down the mirrors, she shimmies out of her clothes and rinses off the grime of the day. Catharsis of hot water and steam—sweat, dust, latex powder, the lemony scent of cleansers, the matching aches in her heels and shoulders—all carried down the polished chrome drain. She dresses, whips her hair up into a messy wet bun, and presses her lips to the mirror, a kiss to her own reflection. Before she leaves, she wipes this little imprint of herself away, swirls her kiss into the glass.

Gina arrives just as Chinta lays the vacuum cleaner in the backseat. Chinta hears Gina's tinkling bracelets before she sees her. She's used to that.

"Girl!" Gina caws from the driveway. "We got to get you a man to do this lifting." She's round and thick all over, her eyebrows drawn on and her hair gelled into a mass of thin wet ringlets sprouting from her head.

"You wanna go find me a decent one? I'm always looking," Chinta says as they give a quick hug. A few strands are caught in Gina's menagerie of gold hoops, and Chinta pulls one out like a thread through a stitch.

"You see what this is doin'? It's so bad. You got to fix what God has done to me!" She laughs as they walk up to the house. "I got rescheduled for the morning shift, and the wet shit takes too long," Gina says, and perches on the windowsill. "I got to be at Dino's by 5:30 so I can serve them old-ass motherfuckers their early-bird special. Can you believe that?" Gina huffs from the heat, her eyes big and indignant. "I sure as hell can't."

"Everybody needs eight hours," Chinta breathes. "If the world wasn't allowed to start until ten, think how much happier everyone would be."

The front door opens and shuts behind them. "Hello, hello," they hear in the hallway, and in swaggers David, still in black slacks and beige work tie, but with stunner shades on and a cigar behind his ear.

"¡Suavecito! Where'd you park?" Chinta pokes him in the stomach when he comes up to give her a hug.

"Why, you got the neighbors on your ass already?" He giggles. David points to his black Accord a few houses down the block. He'd gotten her in trouble with the neighbors at the other houses she's had her people over to. David has a knack for his bumper creeping into red zones and driveways, and the last thing Chinta needs is the neighbors coming up to the door to demand that someone move their car, then crane their neck into the house—as if they have a right—and ask Chinta with suspicion, "What kind of party you got going on in here?" So Chinta takes precautions when she has people at one of her sister's houses. If there's a "For Sale" sign posted in the front yard already, she takes it down. She has her compadres park on the main streets instead of in front of the house she's taking care of. If her cell phone rings, everyone knows to shut up until it's clear if it's Christy or not.

David asks Chinta about the house, if she knows the price appraisal, what the lot size is, but she doesn't know any of those particulars.

"Ask Christy. All that shit is her end of things," she says. "She's the brains. I'm the beauty," she says, and pivots in circles across the shiny hardwood.

They hover in the breeze coming through the window. David complains about the traffic from Walnut Creek. Gina keeps on about the early shift at the restaurant and how one of the new waitresses thinks she's too good to serve burgers and ham and eggs. Chinta takes her turn and complains about the car's AC, how it spits hot air at her, but it will take another three paychecks from Tammy's before she can get the money together to get it fixed. Worst time of the year for it, everyone agrees.

Chinta gathers up the last of her cleansers and dust rags from the front room and lugs them out to her car. Slumping the crates into the back, she then fishes out the green and purple gym bag with her tools inside. Then she wrestles a plain folding chair from the backseat and returns to the house. Gina is breaking down a cigar, splitting its paper skin and emptying out the brown guts onto a magazine in her lap. Everyone chips in a nug for the blunt, and they all squat on the stoop in the backyard and smoke. For a very brief moment, in the middle of David coughing and Gina slapping his back and the smoke swirling around her fingers, Chinta feels like a kid again, like they have just ditched class and have the whole afternoon in front of them to do whatever they please. She passes the blunt and wipes away the drying sweep of sweat on her neck.

She positions the folding chair in the middle of the kitchen, using the new kitchen island as a surface for all of her tools: scissors and clippers, combs and clips, the electric razor and her straight razor (her new favorite tool, perfect for feathering and layering with a single, well-placed draw of the hand), as well as her spray bottles and pomades and relaxers. She leaves the curling iron in the gym bag but plugs in the blow-dryer and flat iron. The tiles alternate in deep indigo and seaweed green, with a little yellow tile thrown in here and there. Lining up her scissors, she likes that she is the first to use this kitchen island.

Gina sits down first, and Chinta throws out her black plastic apron like Zorro throws out his cape and secures it around Gina's fleshy neck. Running her short fingers through her friend's sticky gelled hair, she considers the thickness and texture. "So what you want today?"

Some of her compadres come to get something drastic. Cindy always wants highlights, and the last time Gina came around, she wanted feathered sections and bright red tips. Some of them come and get a trim just to toss her some bills, and Chinta always returns the favor. She will go to Leti to get her nails done or go to the bar Elsie works at when she's on shift. If Chinta needs extra hands to clean up a house, most of her compadres are happy to help her finish up for fifty dollars, and they get to talk shit and laugh and gossip, and afterward, relax with a smoke or a drink in the house freshly cleaned and ready for some stranger to move into.

She's halfway done with Gina when Leti and her friend come through the door with black plastic bags at their wrists, filled with chips and sodas and cigars and Popsicles from the liquor store. Leti comes over, grabs Gina's shoulders, and brays, "No more highlights, girl! Promise me that!"

Gina cocks an eyebrow, but everyone is busting up, so she laughs and tells Leti what a sweet bitch she is.

"Look who I brought to meet you," Leti says, and motions to her friend. The new girl is platform-shoe tall with blond hair and a tattoo of a peacock creeping up the side of her neck. She's the only one in the room wearing silver. "This is Viv. She just started over at my place. She's talking about cutting all this hair off, and I told her you could hook it up," Leti says, and plays with a lock of Viv's hair. Chinta nods at them, refocusing her attention on the comb tracks sectioning Gina's scalp.

The two find a spot to sit on the windowsill. Chinta makes a few minor adjustments to Gina's new layers and holds her hand mirror out for Gina to look. She sees Gina's brown eyes smile in the mirror. The eyes never lie from this angle, Chinta knows that much.

"Just right," Gina says, turning her head right and left, admiring the new shaft of bangs that frames her face. She gets up and slips a twenty into Chinta's palm as they pass. Chinta tucks the bill into her shorts pocket and slaps the metal chair. "David, you're up."

Listening to the chatter of voices and the razor buzzing in her hand, she pretends she's not cutting her compadre's hair in an empty house. The white walls become the creamy walls of her shop, the boom box in the corner turns into a streamlined stereo system with speakers at each corner of the room. She imagines the Lysol smell is really peroxide. She taps her right foot on the imaginary stool pedal, as if to bring her client's head into her waiting hands. Looking at her compadres leaning against the walls and perched on windowsills, she pretends they are lined up in a row in white leather chairs, fluffing their hair and leafing through magazines, waiting for her to work her magic on them.

"Can you take it up a bit?"

"Can you layer it in the back like you did last time?"

"Do what you want. Just make it fabulous!"

She smiles, taps their bills into her back pocket, pretending that her friends' compliments are coming out of the mouths of strangers.

Her ex-boyfriend bought her a miniature barber pole for Christmas, a two-foot-tall electric version with flashing lights that blinked red and white and blue, the colors revolving up and up, endlessly. Everyone says it's tacky, that she's not a barber anyway, but she loves it. He said it was for her shop, when she had her own place. She plugged it in and watched those shards of electric color whirl around and around. Some days, she thinks she'll make it, that once she gets enough money together between these houses and her wages at Tammy's and all the other hustles she has from day to day, somehow it will all come together to get a chair in a good salon. Maybe one day she can have her own little shop: "Chinta's Fabulous Hair and Nails" painted in orange on the storefront windows. But some days, she scrubs and rings up and drives and tries not to think about how cutting hair for her friends is the closest she gets to doing what she loves. She doesn't make enough to rent a chair, and Tammy's doesn't get enough walk-in traffic for Chinta to rent a chair and luck out every month. She holds down the register, ringing up overpriced shampoo and gaudy plastic accessories, and hears every cut of hair—that soft snip of the scissor blades meeting—and wishes she were behind the chair, looking at the customer who meets her gaze in the mirror, surrounded by stage bulbs.

Leti's friend stands up as soon as David is done. Chinta watches her hair move as she walks across the floor. The hair is long for its own sake and brittle from a few too many at-home dye jobs. Shifting in the blond are shocks of faded pink midway down the hair shaft. Once she's in the chair, Chinta considers the straight blond hair falling down the girl's back. "So what were you thinking? Something short?"

Viv touches a lock hanging around her shoulder. "I don't even know what to do with it right now. I've been growing it out for what seems like forever." She cranes her neck back a little, and a tiny stud in her nostril catches the light. "It's time for something new. I just don't know what."

Chinta tests the girl's hair, baby fine strands that fall limp through her fingers. She comes around to the front of the chair, pushes the front sections of Viv's hair off to the left side, then to the right, holding the hair loose between her fingers.

"You've had this mane forever, huh, girl?" Chinta twists a section to see if there's any natural curl. Straight as straw, ragged ends, but in the middle, lots of bounce. Viv nods, and Chinta continues to walk around her in the chair, assessing, considering.

Chinta steps back, puts her hands on her hips. "How brave are you feeling today?" she asks, her eyebrow cocking up.

Viv looks up at her. "What you got for me?"

"You've got the best heart-shaped face, and all this old long hair is just hiding your gorgeous jawbone," Chinta says. She gently turns Viv's chin with her fingers. "Your face was made for a bob."

Viv rolls her eyes. "My grandma has a bob. I want something fresh." Viv tugs at the lock of her hair over her shoulder, and Chinta reaches toward it, guides it around her ear and against the line of her throat. Chinta takes her hand mirror and props it against the counter, positioning it so Viv can see herself. Then she takes her place behind the chair and folds the rest of Viv's hair away so that she can look at herself.

"Look at this angle right here," Chinta says as she draws her finger along the girl's jawline, almost touching her. "If we cut away all this dead hair at the ends, all the hair on top will just fluff up." She draws all the hair away from Viv's neck. "And I'm a give you some layers so some of these colors back here pop again. I can touch the color up for you next time. But for the front…" Chinta gently pulls at the lock of hair curling along her neck. "I can give you a nice shock of hair right here, shape it all into a swoop around, like this. Gonna make everyone notice your neck, your shoulders." Chinta stands back, admiring her vision of what Viv would be. "And if you hate it, I fix it."

Viv's eyes flick between Chinta's reflection and her own. She could see the decision wheels turning in the girl's mind, the curious possibilities with a new look, a new profile, a new self to become. Her cheeks rise up into a smile. "Okay. I'm ready for something different. Leti swears by you, so let's do it."

She takes Viv's hair in both hands, considering where the first cut should be, if she should layer or keep the whole facade straight and sleek. Chinta fluffs Viv's hair again.

"Oh, trust me, we're gonna glam you up! You gonna love it." They both laugh, and Chinta grabs her sheers and a spray bottle, wetting the blond locks until they clump in brown strands. She works a comb through the wet hair, and she senses Viv holding her breath, how her shoulders are tight and her lips pursed.

"You ready to be fabulous?" Chinta pulls the section of hair out, and Viv nods. She cuts the dead hair off, and Viv exhales loudly. She pinches the lock and gives it to the girl, who seems to weigh those seven rust-blond inches in her hands.

Chinta works. She cuts. She measures twice with her fingers before each snip. Bits of damp clippings fall around Chinta's feet, little bursts of cool damp on the tops of her feet. Viv plays with the bundle of her dead hair in her hands while Chinta works. She double-checks the new line of her hair, straight and clean as a blade, and makes sure that the line follows Viv's jaw. She sculpts the cut in the back and begins to tailor the swath of long hair from the nape of her neck to just below her left ear, working the lengths to affect a loose tendril of locks that will curl down the hollow of her neck. She didn't hear her phone go off, much less the car horn. It wasn't until Leti tugged at her shoulder that she undid herself from that falling fold of hair.

"Christy's pulling into the driveway." Leti whispers into Chinta's ear. Her fingers seize in the scissors, thankfully far from Viv's hair. David and Gina have gathered their Coke cans and jackets, and Leti's eyes are stuck on the green minivan that is inching toward Chinta's car in the driveway. The Realtor's wheel sign has been slapped onto the sliding door—a fifty-fifty chance that Christy will walk through the front door with a prospect or an associate. Christy only comes to houses on business.

Her compadres all look to her. The engine outside idles, then shuts off. Viv holds her head perfectly still. She reeks of weed and hair products.

Chinta motions toward the back porch. "Out the back way, there's a side fence to the street. Just cut," she says low to Gina and David. She turns to Leti. "We'll be out in five minutes. She's practically done. Just kick it in your car a minute." Her voice is calm and smooth, the opposite of her heart, which suddenly seems far too big to be contained in her chest.

Finally, she turns back to Viv. She holds her purse in her lap. "What's the problem?"

Chinta shakes her head. "No problem. My sister's here, that's all. Don't worry, I'm gonna finish you up. I'm taking care of you right now." The sun has moved through the telephone wires, bisected into two burning halves by the trunks of telephone poles. The whole room is filled with the red gold light of summer afternoon. At Chinta's feet, the clippings from Viv's hair curl into golden feathers on the floor.

What sounds like steps begin to muffle their way up the concrete walk outside. Gina and David make their way out the back porch to the street, giggling like teenagers. Leti hangs back, unwilling to abandon her friend midcut. Instead, she grabs Chinta's duffel bag and motions to the tools laid out. "Want me to stash all this?"

"Leave them." Chinta keeps her eyes trained on Viv's hair, trying to keep her focus. "I need my tools."

Leti slinks into the hallway in between the kitchen and the back door. Chinta considers her sister, the house she is in, this lock of hair in her hands. Her heart stops racing, slows like her breath, like the slow whirl of the barber pole that swirls day and night in her room.

She hears the keys in the lock, the slow grind of the hinge as her sister comes plodding into the entryway. She can make out her tall brown hair and ridiculous shoulder pads in the periphery, registers her voice. Something like, What are you doing? What the hell is this? What What Why Who What Are You Doing?

"I'm working." Shears in hand, she smiles at Viv, who smiles back, and takes the last section of hair between her forefingers. The scissors snap across the final blades of hair. The open windows leave no shadows across their faces as the sun pours in, flowing out into the dark-red floorboards, a warm red pool of light around them that seems to never, ever spill.

ACKNOWLEDGMENTS

Inspiration is private, but art is made in a community, and I am indebted to my community of writers in the Bay Area, in LA, in the islands, and in all the places that can't be mapped. This book wouldn't have come into being without your generosity, your insights, and your support. Thank you to Malcolm Margolin, Gayle Wattawa, and all the folks at Heyday for reading my work with such care. Thank you to my teachers, who continue to guide me as a craftsperson: Steve Guttierrez, Susan Gubernat, Susan Straight, Michael Jayme Becerra, and Chris Abani. Thank you to my readers at UCR. Thank you especially to Jackie Bang and Amir Friedlander, who always had coffee, questions, beautiful words, and time to read another draft. Thank you to Ed Kalafus, Joseph Kurz, and Daniel Schneider, for your love and confidence in that final push. Thank you to Gary Kubota, for all of your advice. Of course, thank you to my mother and father and brother and nephew. Thank you to my Bay family and my island ohana—the water in my well.

ABOUT THE AUTHOR

MARIAH K. YOUNG was born in San Leandro and spent her childhood living in the Bay Area and in Lahaina, Hawai'i. She graduated with an English degree from CSU East Bay, where she won the first annual R.V. Williams Fiction Prize. In 2008, she earned her MFA in creative writing from UC Riverside. That year, she attended the Squaw Valley Writers' Workshop on fellowship. She currently lives and teaches writing in Los Angeles.

Photo by Cupid Flowers

About Heyday

Heyday is an independent, nonprofit publisher and unique cultural institution. We promote widespread awareness and celebration of California's many cultures, landscapes, and boundary-breaking ideas. Through our well-crafted books, public events, and innovative outreach programs we are building a vibrant community of readers, writers, and thinkers.

Thank You

It takes the collective effort of many to create a thriving literary culture. We are thankful to all the thoughtful people we have the privilege to engage with. Cheers to our writers, artists, editors, storytellers, designers, printers, bookstores, critics, cultural organizations, readers, and book lovers everywhere!

We are especially grateful for the generous funding we've received for our publications and programs during the past year from foundations and hundreds of individual donors. Major supporters include:

Acorn Naturalists; Alliance for California Traditional Artists; Anonymous; James J. Baechle; Bay Tree Fund; S. D. Bechtel Jr., Foundation; Barbara Jean and Fred Berensmeier; Joan Berman; Buena Vista Rancheria; Lewis and Sheana Butler; California Civil Liberties Public Education Program, California State Library; California Council for the Humanities; The Keith Campbell Foundation; Center for California Studies; Jon Christensen; The Christensen Fund; Berkeley Civic Arts Program and Civic Arts Commission; Compton Foundation; Lawrence Crooks; Nik Dehejia; Frances Dinkelspiel and Gary Wayne; Troy Duster; Euclid Fund at the East Bay Community Foundation; Mark and Tracy Ferron; Judith Flanders; Karyn and Geoffrey Flynn; Furthur Foundation; The Fred Gellert Family Foundation; Wallace Alexander Gerbode Foundation; Nicola W. Gordon; Wanda Lee Graves and Stephen Duscha; Alice

Getting Involved

To learn more about our publications, events, membership club, and other ways you can participate, please visit www.heydaybooks.com.

James D. Houston Award Donors

Heyday wishes to thank the following individuals, foundations, and corporations for their generous support of the James D. Houston Award:

Barbara Adair; Dugan Aguilar; Linda Allen; Anonymous; James J. Baechle; Tandy Beal and Jonathan Scoville; M. Melanie Beene; Ralph Benson; Edwin Bernbaum; Claire Biancalana; Rita and Thomas Bottoms; Roberta Bristol; Julianne Burton-Carvajal; Gail Canyon Sam; Bessie Chin; Lawrence Coates; Kathleen Croughan; Peter Dahl; H. Dwight Damon; Sylvia De Trinidad; John and Harriet Deck; Sandra Dijkstra; George and Kathleen Diskant; Amy Doherty; Laurel Douglass; Paul and Charlene Douglass; Glenn J. Farris; Liudmila Finney; Judith Flanders; Rebecca Foster; R. Dennis Fritzinger; Maria Gitin; Jan Goggans; Hilary Goldstine; Jane Gregorius; Alice Guild; Charles Haas; Joell Hallowell; Masaru and Marcia Hashimoto; Gerald and Jan Haslam; Hawaii Sons, Inc., The Brian and Patricia A. Herman Fund at Community Foundation Santa Cruz County; Jack Hicks; Carla Hills; Donna Hoenig-Couch; George Hong; G. Scott Hong Charitable Trust; D. Tomi Kobara; Arnold Kotler; Michael Kowalewski; Joe M. Lamb; Elinor Langer; Jacqeline and Homer Lohr; Laura Louis; Susan Maresco; Judy McAfee and John Mikols; Mary McGrath; Virginia and David McGuire; Joyce Milligan; Clare Morris; Scott Morrison; Nam Hee Mun; Victoria Myers; James and Carlin Naify; Thad Nodine and Shelby Graham; Regina Ockelmann; Rodney A. Ohtani; Charlotte Painter; Theresa Park; Gerri Pedesky; Daniel and Judith Phillips; Kathleen Marie Pouls; Madeleine Provost; Richard Reinhardt; James and Janet Reynolds; Fred Setterberg and Ann Van Steenberg; Victoria Shoemaker; Susan Snyder and Richard Neidhardt; Robin Somers; Tom Sourisseau Jr.; Byron and Lee Stookey; Craig Strang and Persis Karim; Barbara Tannenbaum; John C. Thorland; Andrew Tonkovich; Kerry Tremain; Gail Tsukiyama; Eugene Unger; Daniel Urbach; Louis Warren; M.C. Winkley; Jane Yamashiro; Andrea Yee; Stan Yogi and David Carroll; and Ruth S. Young.